THE MIRAC

Lisa Bingham

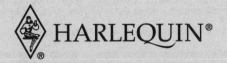

HARLEQUIN®

TORONTO • NEW YORK • LONDON
AMSTERDAM • PARIS • SYDNEY • HAMBURG
STOCKHOLM • ATHENS • TOKYO • MILAN • MADRID
PRAGUE • WARSAW • BUDAPEST • AUCKLAND

To my own miracle children and the three incredible
birth mothers who gave them life.

ISBN 0-373-75036-6

THE MIRACLE TWINS

Copyright © 2004 by Lisa Bingham Rampton.

This edition published by arrangement with Harlequin Books S.A.

www.eHarlequin.com

Printed in U.S.A.

"Why are you here, Lucy?" Nick asked quietly

"I need help."

The words were offered so grudgingly that he might have smiled if she'd been anyone else.

"From me?" he blurted out in disbelief. A short bark of laughter escaped before he could stop it. "As I recall, we didn't exactly part on good terms. Let's see, you told me you were choosing your job over me, then you ran for the exit."

A flush spread up her neck and over her cheeks. "What happened in the past is hardly relevant."

"It seemed damned relevant to me at the time," he countered.

"You've got to hear me out," Lucy said urgently. "Please." She reached into her pocket and withdrew a photograph.

It took a moment for Nick to absorb what he was seeing. The photo was of two children placed close enough together that their bodies touched and appeared to be entwined. No, not entwined.

Conjoined.

Bit by bit, the significance of Lucy's visit began to sink in. Nick knew instinctively that she hadn't come to him merely for advice. She wanted more than that. Much more.

Dear Reader,

The premise for *The Miracle Twins* came to me while I spent a week in the intermediate care nursery at a local hospital with my first daughter. I was so impressed by the many doctors and nurses who had dedicated their careers to the welfare of children. Even more touching were the doting parents who spent countless hours rocking these tiny infants or keeping watch over high-tech isolettes until the day they were allowed to bring their children home.

I hope you enjoy *The Miracle Twins*. My readers have been a source of so much joy to me. I want to thank you for all the support you've sent my way.

All best,

Lisa Bingham

Chapter One

As she settled into a taxi and left the Salt Lake City International Airport behind her, Lucy Devon decided that she didn't appreciate life's little ironies. No matter how hard she tried to make thoughtful, well-planned decisions, her mistakes had a way of coming back to haunt her. "Never say never," her mother had been fond of quoting. "God is always listening."

"Too true, Mom," Lucy whispered under her breath as the cab began to climb upward toward the eastern bench of the Wasatch Mountains.

From this vantage point, she had a beautiful view of the city. As dusk fell, lights began to twinkle like gold dust in the gathering gloom. If she tried hard enough, Lucy was sure she could find the tall, copper-colored building where she'd completed her journalism internship as a graduate student at the

University of Utah. The university was where she and Nick Hammond had first met and fallen in love. And it was over there, a few more blocks to the east, that she'd decided marrying him would ruin all chances of furthering her career.

Dear God, had she really gone to the courthouse just before their wedding to tell him she was rejecting him in favor of "the story of a lifetime"?

Even now, the thought of those few tempestuous minutes could make her squirm in embarrassment and shame. Try as she might, she hadn't been able to wipe away the memory of the expressions that had come over his face one after the other: disbelief, disgust and then anger. After making her escape, Lucy had sworn that, as long as she lived, she would never see Nick again. She wouldn't go even a hundred miles near the place Nick lived and worked.

"But God has other plans," she breathed.

"Did you say something, miss?" the cabdriver asked, glancing over his shoulder.

Lucy grimaced. "No. Just talking to myself."

The man chose to let the comment pass. "You got family you're visiting here in town?"

She made a noncommittal noise.

"That's nice," the driver said absently, his attention on the road.

Nice wasn't exactly the word Lucy would have

used to explain her current predicament. She would've done anything to avoid the upcoming meeting.

The cabdriver pointed to a house on the corner. "That's the address up there."

The taxi pulled to a stop at the curb, and Lucy peered through the window. Lights blazed from the house and the distant thump of music could be heard over the running engine.

The driver ducked to see the brass numbers bolted to the cottage-style rock home perched on a slight knoll. "Yep. This is it."

"How much do I owe you?" Lucy asked, opening her purse.

"Eleven-fifty."

She gave him fifteen dollars with a murmured, "Keep the change." Then, opening the door, she ignored her twisting stomach and stepped onto the verdant strip of grass that bordered the curb. After a moment's pause, the taxi rolled away, then disappeared entirely behind a bend in the road.

Instantly, Lucy felt oh, so alone.

A soft breeze caressed her cheek, the cool, moist air a harbinger of spring. As she walked up the terraced path, Lucy noticed that the trees were still skeletal. But the fuzzy tips of a pussy willow near the front stoop gave ample testimony that winter was losing its grip. Lucy had always loved spring. In her mind, it was a time for new beginnings.

So why was she about to dredge up the past?

Making a face, Lucy knew she'd had little choice. Nick Hammond was a spectacular surgeon, and right now she needed his skills.

What will he think when he sees me on his doorstep? Will he smile?

"More likely, he'll kick you off the premises," she told herself. Then, knowing there was no point in avoiding the inevitable, she started up the steps.

So much had happened to bring her to this point—and so much rested on the next few minutes. There was no plan B. If Nick refused to help her, she didn't know what she'd do.

He *had* to help her. Nick had never been a petty man. He wouldn't send her away without hearing her out.

At least…she *hoped* he wouldn't send her away.

As she lifted her hand to ring the bell, Lucy prayed she could keep her wits about her for just a little longer. Her temples throbbed from a killer case of jet lag. Worse yet, she was trapped in a time warp; her mind moved sluggishly and her motor skills were only slightly better.

Don't think about that now. Think about the children and only the children.

Straightening her shoulders in renewed determination she passed a hand over her short hair, and pressed the doorbell. From deep within the house, she could hear the sound reverberating.

As she waited for the door to be answered, Lucy recited the same litany she'd repeated a thousand times since leaving Africa. *Nick is a reasonable man. A professional. Once you've explained your predicament, he's bound to help you. He would never let the past interfere.*

Or would he?

They hadn't parted on the best of terms. Nick had felt humiliated, while Lucy—

When Lucy had turned to walk away from Nick, the judge and the witnesses, Lucy had seen the main door like a trapped animal who'd spied a hole in the fence. The moment she was out of sight of the wedding party, she'd started to run.

And she'd been running from the memory ever since.

No. She wouldn't think about that now. The past was past, and the decision she'd made to cancel her wedding had been the right one. Lucy wasn't the "marrying kind"—and she'd proven that to herself time and time again. She grew jittery and uncomfortable if she stayed in one place too long. The pressures of her job, the travel and risk involved, didn't lend themselves to even the most casual of relationships, let alone marriage.

Wrenching her thoughts back to the matter at hand, Lucy scowled. Lights blazed from most of the windows. Yet several minutes had gone by and no one had appeared.

Ringing the doorbell again, Lucy cursed the fact that she hadn't asked the cabdriver to wait. With her luck, she'd come all this way only to be marooned until Nick returned from some emergency at the hospital. True, she had her cell phone, but after gathering enough courage to face Nick tonight, she didn't plan on leaving until she'd seen him.

Irritated, Lucy pressed the doorbell a third time, keeping her finger on the button for several seconds. Then she punctuated her imperious summons by banging the brass door knocker.

"Where is he?" she muttered.

Abruptly she froze, knowing that any minute the door would open and she would be face-to-face with Nick Hammond, the only man who'd ever made her knees quake.

What would be her reaction after all these years? Would she still feel an instant tug of attraction?

No. It wasn't possible. Too much time had passed. She wasn't the same woman she'd been then. Her experiences had hardened her. She couldn't possibly—

The door flew open and Lucy's heart stopped in her chest, then began a slow, sluggish beat.

This was the man she'd refused to marry?

A hot tide seeped into her cheeks and she was infused with embarrassment. She'd obviously interrupted Nick in the middle of a shower. He stood before her wearing nothing but a robe, his hair dark and spiky with moisture. Water dappled his bare skin, stray droplets streaking his chest.

A bolt of heat shot through her body and settled low in her abdomen. She swallowed against the dryness gathering in her throat, knowing that if she tried to talk, her voice would emerge as a croak.

"Lucy?"

Her name was a mere breath of sound, but it brushed her senses like a caress.

Talk to him, idiot. Say something. You can't stand here gaping at the man.

"Nick." His name was garbled and barely audible, and she cleared her throat. "Hello."

To his credit, Nick kept his composure. In fact, other than the slight tightening of his fingers around his belt, he appeared completely unaffected by her sudden arrival. His features smoothed into an expressionless mask and his eyes became hooded, giving nothing away.

Why didn't he say something? Why did he keep

looking at her as if she had suddenly appeared from an alien planet?

Lucy thrust her hands into the pockets of her jacket, shivering in the cool spring air. But it wasn't the chill of spring that caused her skin to tingle. As his gaze slipped down her body, gooseflesh pebbled her skin. Lucy tried to meet his inspection with one of her own, but as she absorbed the sight of his nearly naked body, she knew she would be a fool to continue. Her mind might insist that she was over her college infatuation, but her body had a different idea.

Fastening her eyes on the faint cleft in his chin, she refused to look down. She was only concerned with his mind and his hands, the main tools of a surgeon.

Liar.

When the silence grew even more uncomfortable, Lucy said, "Are you going to let me in?"

Nick's gaze intensified—as if he was trying to divine the reason for her sudden appearance. But finally he stepped back, making a sweeping gesture with his arm.

"Be my guest."

Lucy brushed past him into a narrow entry hall. As she did so, she was inundated with the scents of shampoo and soap.

Not for the first time, Lucy rued the fact that she'd been forced to come to Nick for help. She'd investigated several other surgeons. But whenever she'd reviewed her list, she'd known that Nick was her only real choice.

So she'd taken a flight to Salt Lake City, insisting to herself that the past didn't have any bearing on her current mission. She'd eventually begun to believe that she could deal with Nick in a manner that was both friendly and detached.

But now she wasn't so sure.

You're tired, that's all. Weariness can do funny things to a person.

"Take a seat in the living room."

He pointed at a small space to her right. White walls and a minimum of furniture offered a slightly neglected appearance—as if Nick spent as little time in his home as she did in her apartment in Chicago. It was a bachelor's domain, dominated by a huge sound-and-television system, a battered recliner and a table piled high with medical journals. There were no telltale signs of a woman—no bric-a-brac, no photographs, no hint of lace or flowers.

Lucy couldn't deny that his single status—if she'd guessed correctly—would make matters easier. She was about to infringe on Nick's time in a completely overbearing way, and she didn't need a jealous wife impatiently tapping her toe in the background.

Stepping into the sunken living room, Lucy turned to face Nick. Since he'd remained in the entry hall, she was forced to look up, up, before meeting his dark gaze.

"Nice place," she said, even though the older home wasn't at all what she'd expected from a successful surgeon. She had been so sure she'd find him living in a mansion above the Avenues, not a cul-de-sac near Westminster College.

"What are you doing here, Lucy?"

So much for chitchat.

She opened her mouth to speak, but before she could utter a sound, he held up one hand.

"No. Wait here. I need to get dressed first."

Turning on his heel, he'd taken two of the carpeted steps before she asked, "Do you often answer the door in your bathrobe?"

Immediately, she wished she'd kept her mouth shut. As he peered at her over the railing, a tingling awareness shot down her spine. She became uncomfortably conscious of the white terry cloth, which revealed part of his chest and the slick wetness of his skin. Nick's body was more powerful than she remembered, the muscles sculpted and well defined—yet another reason for her to believe he was unmarried. In her experience, married men usually didn't have much time to devote to a rigorous training schedule in a gym.

But that didn't mean he was unattached. There might not be a Mrs. Hammond, but chances were that Nick was involved with *someone*.

"I was expecting a colleague from the hospital with some urgent reports."

"I see." But even though the explanation seemed reasonable, she wondered if he was telling the truth. Maybe Nick was giving her an excuse so that he wouldn't have to admit he was waiting for someone else. Someone who wouldn't mind being greeted in such a familiar manner.

She was tempted to blurt out her suspicions, but before she could say a thing, Nick climbed the rest of the stairs and disappeared from view.

"That went well," she grumbled under her breath.

Removing her hands from her pockets, she wiped them down the legs of her jeans, damning the moisture that revealed her nervousness. Try as she might, she couldn't push away the image of Nick standing in the stairwell, the overhead light bathing his skin in a layer of gold.

Pull yourself together, Lucy, she inwardly chided. She'd come to Nick to ask him for his help as a surgeon.

He could never be anything more to her than that.

NICK HAMMOND SLAMMED his bedroom door behind him, dropped the robe on the floor and cursed softly under his breath.

When he'd heard the doorbell through the drumming of the shower, Nick hadn't dreamed that it would be anyone other than Max Garcia. Max was a fellow surgeon who'd wanted a second opinion on the results of some tests for a young patient. If Nick had even thought that Lucy might be waiting on his porch…

She was the *last* person Nick would've expected to see. Five years ago, he'd arrived at the Salt Lake City courthouse intent on marrying her. Lucy's rejection had been an emotional blow. When he'd watched her disappear, he'd been so sure he'd never see her again.

Since then, he'd done his best to push the unpleasant episode into the vague corners of his memory— a task that had proved more difficult than he'd imagined. Within months of leaving him at the courthouse, Lucy had become one of the prime foreign correspondents with CNC. And for a news junkie like Nick, seeing her face on television had been inevitable.

But he'd never expected to find her here. In his own home.

Realizing that his thoughts were circling like a

loop of bad audiotape, Nick dragged on underwear, a faded sweatshirt, jeans, socks and a pair of battered running shoes. Then, after raking his fingers through his short hair, he took a deep, calming breath.

Yes, he'd been stunned to see her, but the surprise was over. So there was no need for his body to maintain the tension it had adopted the moment he'd seen her cool green eyes and angular features. He wasn't in love with Lucy anymore. In fact, he'd begun to wonder if he'd ever been in love with her. He'd been able to convince himself that his emotional involvement had been like too much wine—a brief, powerful intoxication that had worn off with time. So when his body had immediately slipped into the rush of attraction he'd once experienced in Lucy's presence, he'd been momentarily taken aback. But he was in control of his thoughts and his emotions now.

Whipping open the door, he hurried down the staircase, only to stop halfway. Lucy stood in his living room, gazing out the window, obviously unaware of his arrival.

For a moment, he was struck by the droop of her shoulders and the protective way she hugged her arms to her chest. In the light streaming from the hall, she seemed pale and much too thin. Her green eyes dominated her face.

"You look like hell, Lucy."

She started, and he watched as she donned an expression of hauteur.

"It's nice to see you, too."

He joined her in the living room. "What have you been doing with yourself?"

She shrugged. "I'm a reporter."

"I know. I've seen you on television. You have a very impressive career."

"As do you."

Moving toward her, Nick had the distinct impression that his nearness bothered her. He sensed her tension as the space between them disappeared, but despite her discomfort, she held her ground.

Closer, Nick decided that she looked downright haggard. She was at least ten pounds underweight. Her skin was drawn tightly over her cheekbones, making her features seem that much more angular and exotic.

And vulnerable. Much too vulnerable for a thirty-six-year-old woman who had already been through more in her short career than others would be in a lifetime.

Shaking away the thought, Nick slid his hands into his pockets.

"Why are you here, Lucy?" he asked quietly.

Lucy assumed a look of bravado that she patently didn't feel.

"I need help, Nick."

The words were offered so grudgingly that he might have smiled if she'd been anyone else.

"From *me?*" he blurted in disbelief. A short bark of laughter escaped before he could stop it.

Lucy frowned. "You needn't sound so shocked."

She was so obviously wounded by his affront that he laughed again.

"And why not? As I recall, we didn't exactly part on good terms. Let's see, you told me you were choosing your job over me, then you ran for the exit."

A flush spread up her neck and over her cheeks. "What happened in the past is hardly relevant."

"It seemed damn relevant to me at the time," he countered.

"A lot of years have passed since then."

"Five, to be precise."

She sighed. "I haven't come here to rehash the past."

"Then why *are* you here?"

She hesitated for an awkward beat of silence. Then she lifted her chin and announced, "I need a favor that only you can grant."

His eyebrows rose. "What's wrong? Couldn't find a date for the Emmys so you're falling back on an old relationship?"

Her cheeks burned even more and she clenched her fists, but her voice remained calm and even. "No.

I need your help with a professional matter and you're the only person I can trust."

Nick snorted. He should have known. She'd come for a story, nothing more.

"I'm sorry, I don't give interviews."

"I haven't come for an interview."

He rocked back on his heels, eyeing her suspiciously. "Then what *do* you want?"

"I need your help with a…medical matter."

For the first time, Nick was forced to acknowledge that Lucy's pallor might be a result of something other than mere vanity. Was Lucy ill? The thought was more disturbing that he cared to admit.

Instantly, he was swamped by the urge to protect her, but he pushed the sensation away in self-disgust. He'd experienced those same emotions before, and look where they'd taken him.

"I'm a pediatric surgeon," he said bluntly. "You're a little old for my specialty."

"I know."

When she continued to watch him with pleading ice-green eyes, the full meaning of her response sank into his brain. "You have…a *child* with a problem?"

"Yes."

She was married.

Or not. Women didn't necessarily marry these days in order to have a baby.

Still, the image of Lucy with a child was unsettling. He'd assumed that she was single and unfettered by family ties. Call it hubris, but he'd believed that if she wouldn't marry him, she wouldn't marry anyone.

A baby. His hands curled into fists and he fought the tension gathering in his stomach.

"No." His response was low and curt.

"No?" she echoed blankly.

"No, I can't help you. It wouldn't be a good idea."

"*Can't* or *won't?*"

"I won't help you," he said firmly. Any prolonged contact he might have would only breed more trouble.

Nick turned, making his way toward the door.

"Wait!" She reached out, stopping him. "You haven't even heard what I have to say."

Her touch was like a firebrand and his reaction was visceral and complete. Damn it all, hadn't he learned anything? The sexual attraction between them had always been intense and instantaneous. But there was no substance to their emotions, nothing other than passion. They'd never had what it took to make a truly lasting relationship. That had been the most painful truth he'd had to acknowledge five years earlier. Eventually he'd seen that it was better the two of them hadn't married. They'd each been too independent and too self-absorbed to sustain anything but a passionate affair.

"You've got to hear me out," Lucy said urgently, tugging on his arm. "Please." She reached into her pocket and withdrew a photograph. "This is the reason I've come to you for help."

Chapter Two

It took a moment for Nick to absorb what he was seeing. The photo was of two children placed close
enough together that their bodies touched and appeared to be entwined. No, not entwined.

Conjoined.

As Nick peered at the picture, he could see that
the tiny, naked bodies were fused from the breast-
bone to the abdomen. Otherwise, the little girls, no
more than a few weeks old, looked fairly healthy, if
a little underweight.

He was so absorbed in studying the twins that he
couldn't even remember how he'd come to be holding the photograph. "Where did you get this?"

"The children—the twins—have been placed in
my care."

His forehead creased. The twins were dark as the
finest chocolate. Wisps of black fluff dusted the tops

of their heads and eyes bright as new coins stared curiously in the direction of the camera's lens. Judging by the clarity of the shot and the haunting quality of the image, the photo had probably been taken by Lucy. During her undergraduate studies, she'd made a name for herself with her stark portrait photography—a sideline job that had helped Lucy pay her way through college.

With a wave of shame, Nick realized that Lucy had been honest in insisting that she'd come to him for medical reasons rather than personal ones. He could only imagine how much it had cost her pride to approach him.

Nevertheless, as he traced a thumb over the photograph, a part of Nick urged him to say no once again and send Lucy on her way. He'd be a fool to put himself into a position of working closely with her. But even as he considered refusing, he knew the children's plight couldn't be ignored.

"Where were they born?"

"In Zaire, in a village along the Congo River. They were left in an orphanage after their mother died in childbirth."

"How old are they?"

"Nearly three months."

"They're awfully small for three months."

"They are underweight for their age. When their

mother died, the hospital had a hard time obtaining breast milk. The children have had some difficulties adjusting to formula. A good portion of their food has to be administered through a feeding tube."

Bit by bit, the significance of Lucy's visit began to sink in. Nick knew instinctively that Lucy hadn't come to him merely for advice. She wanted more than that. Much more.

"You're here to see if they can be separated."

It wasn't a question, but Lucy nodded.

He took a deep breath. "I don't know if I can help."

"Don't say no. Please. I trust you. I trust your skills as a surgeon. You have to examine them at least. I've already made arrangements for their travel. They'll be arriving by chartered plane tomorrow evening."

His eyes narrowed, moving from the picture to Lucy's anxious face. "You took a lot for granted."

"Yes. Yes, I did. I don't want just anyone to operate on them. I want the best. Someone I can trust."

Nick fought the warmth that followed her statements. He found it incredible that after everything that had happened between them, she still felt she could trust him.

Yet she hadn't trusted him enough to marry him.

"Please say you'll consider my request, Nick. That's all I ask."

Nick knew in his gut that he should refer her to another surgeon altogether, but he held back. There was only a handful of pediatric specialists in the country who might be willing to take on an assignment like this.

But as he confronted the hope shining in her eyes, he admitted that his reasons for resisting weren't entirely professional.

Nodding his head, Nick reluctantly agreed. "I'll do a cursory evaluation when they get here, but I can't make any promises about surgery. Not until I've seen them."

Relief flooded her eyes, darkening them to a rich mossy shade. It was those eyes—which changed from icy sage to rich green with her emotions—that had first drawn Nick's attention so long ago. Lucy had once told him she'd never been any good at lying because she couldn't keep her gaze from revealing her true state of mind. Nick was glad to see that moving from one hot spot in the world to another hadn't changed that.

Unable to keep back the words, he murmured, "It *is* good to see you, Lucy."

She suddenly became aware of the palm she'd laid on his forearm. When she would have backed away, he cupped his hand beneath her chin, holding her face up to the light.

"Are you happy?"

He didn't know what had made him ask, but he waited tensely, half dreading her answer. For all he knew, she might reveal that leaving him had been the best thing she'd ever done.

Ignoring his question, she released herself and said, "I'll let you know as soon as I have the twins' exact arrival time."

"Fine."

Knowing Lucy meant to leave, Nick held the picture out of her reach. The expression on her face was so similar to the one she'd worn seconds before she'd darted out of the courthouse five years ago that he experienced a rush of déjà vu.

"Don't go yet. I need to know some specifics on the children so I can check into things at the hospital."

She frowned. Obviously, she dreaded the thought that he might delve into their past relationship. In an attempt to reassure her, he pointed toward his office. "We can talk in there."

She preceded him slowly into the room. As he followed her, Nick wondered why he'd been so insistent on making her stay.

Because you're a fool, that's why.

IT WAS CLOSE TO ten o'clock when Lucy shut the hotel room door behind her, then sagged against the panels.

In her career as a foreign correspondent, she had interviewed kings, potentates and dictators. She'd grilled criminals and mercenaries. But never, ever, had she endured a more uncomfortable two hours.

Summoning what little strength she had left after days of traveling by jeep, bus and airplane—all the while preparing for her upcoming confrontation with Nick—she peeled off her jacket, kicked off her shoes and fell onto the bed face-first.

Sleep. She needed sleep. Perhaps then, she wouldn't cringe when she thought of her embarrassing reaction to the man. It was a testament to her mental weariness that she hadn't been able to control her body's wayward response.

Heaven only knew there was no reason for her to have behaved in such an adolescent fashion. At thirty-six she was too old to grow weak in the knees at the sight of a man with whom she'd once been intimately involved. She should have left as soon as he'd agreed to look at the girls. But something had caused her to linger.

As if she'd been waiting…

For what? For the conversation to become more personal? For a familiar glance? A touch?

Groaning, she pressed the palms of her hands against her eyes. Perhaps the most surprising moment of the evening had come when Nick offered her the use of his guest room. Naturally, she'd refused. Staying at his home would have been too…unsettling. Too dangerous.

Sleep. She needed sleep. A few hours of uninterrupted sleep should be enough to shake off her strange reaction to an old relationship.

Lucy pushed herself up, dragged her suitcase to the foot of the bed and located an oversize T-shirt. Minutes later, she had taken the fastest shower on record and climbed between the sheets.

But the moment her head touched the pillow, her mind began replaying the evening's events. Even more disturbing, her body ached with an unmistakable sensual awareness—one she'd sworn she wouldn't feel again.

Squeezing her eyes shut, Lucy made herself remember all the reasons she'd ended her relationship with Nick years ago.

At the time, Lucy had still been a struggling graduate student intent on becoming a reporter. She'd known that making it to the top of her field would require constant travel, unyielding stress and overt danger. Such a lifestyle would never mesh with Nick's. His profession as a surgeon would entail remaining in one place and leading a life dominated by his own challenging schedule.

But even as she'd insisted that this was why she

couldn't marry him, she'd been aware that there were deeper reasons. Reasons she hadn't fully understood herself, let alone been able to explain to Nick. It had taken her years to understand that part of her motivation for remaining alone and working so hard had been to escape all vestiges of her childhood.

When Lucy was asked how she could tolerate living in a war zone, she was often tempted to tell people that she'd grown up in one. For as long as she could remember, Lucy had felt as if she were a hostage in her own home. She was an only child caught in the battleground of her parents' loveless marriage.

George Devon had been a stern, critical man for whom nothing was ever good enough. He'd ruled his wife and his daughter with an iron hand, dictating what they would wear, what they would eat, how many pennies they would be allotted for their personal needs. He'd demanded immediate and complete obedience.

But George wasn't the only person at fault. Although he'd ordained himself taskmaster of her parents' relationship, her mother had become the self-appointed martyr.

Lucy grimaced. Not one day had gone by without Lucy being reminded of her mother's unhappiness. Lillian had constantly spoken of her woes.

She'd complained about the way she'd denied herself any possibility of following her own dreams in order to keep the marriage from falling apart. Yet in her zeal to retain their conventional family unit, she'd been blind to the fact that her own unhappiness had been as ravaging as George Devon's anger. Year by year, Lucy had watched her mother wither away. Where once she'd been a joyful, loving woman, she'd soon become a sad, embittered ghost of herself. And as she'd descended into despair, she'd brought her daughter along for the ride.

When Lucy had agreed to marry Nick, it hadn't been without misgivings. Her greatest fear had been that she wasn't capable of sustaining a loving relationship. After all, she'd had no role models as a child. She wasn't even sure if she believed in true love. But Nick's exuberance had allowed Lucy to push her own concerns aside.

Lucy groaned, remembering those horrible few weeks leading up to the wedding. With each day that had passed, her worries had increased, not diminished. She'd become paralyzed with fear, certain that she'd fail to measure up to Nick's expectations.

Finally, when she'd been sure she was about to shatter into a million pieces from the stress of it all, Lucy had realized she couldn't be the person Nick wanted her to be. Marriage had felt like an impending prison sentence, personally and professionally. In being totally honest with herself, she'd acknowledged that her drive to succeed was as necessary as breathing. She couldn't live without the thrill of hunting down a story. And she wouldn't subject her loved ones to the pressures her job demanded.

And nothing had changed since then. Nothing at all.

Rolling onto her side, she pounded her pillow into shape with more force than was necessary.

Enough. She wouldn't think about Nick or the past. She had more important concerns to occupy her thoughts—such as two little girls who'd been entrusted to her care.

Tomorrow, the twins would arrive. The nuns from the orphanage had christened them Faith and Hope, and the names fit. Not quite three months old, they had overcome enormous obstacles just to survive. So much was riding on whether or not they could be separated. They deserved the very best medical attention Lucy could provide. She couldn't allow herself to forget that.

THE NEXT EVENING, Nick stood with his palms braced on the shower wall, the hot spray beating down on the cramped muscles of his shoulders.

There had been a time when he could complete a full day of surgery, then play a game or two of basketball at a local gym afterward. But he was beginning to discover that—try as he might to ward off the effects of turning forty with diet and exercise—his stamina wasn't what it used to be.

Granted, the morning hadn't started out well. He'd had his whole day booked before he even stepped through the doors of Primary Children's Medical Center. A six-car pileup on I-15 had resulted in two youngsters being air-lifted to the hospital before dawn. At six, Nick had been in one of the operating theaters, and he hadn't left until after seven that night.

Which meant he was tired. Bone tired.

Normally, after a punishing day Nick treated himself to a quiet evening. He'd turn on some jazz or watch a game on television. But tonight…

Tonight, he felt edgy and anxious. His house was too quiet.

Grimacing at the melancholy turn of his own thoughts, Nick squeezed shampoo into his palm and vigorously scrubbed his scalp. If he was willing to indulge in self-pity, he *was* getting old. Now wasn't the time to—

A muffled noise filtered into his musings. Frowning, Nick stepped away from the spray and bent his

head in the direction of the bathroom door, sure that
he was mistaken. But the muted sound of the doorbell left him in no doubt that someone had chosen
this inopportune moment to visit.

Cursing, he rinsed the soap out of his hair, shut off
the water and grabbed a towel. Max Garcia still hadn't
dropped off the case study, and it was possible that
Nick's colleague was waiting on the stoop, but Nick
doubted it. Instinctively, he knew the identity of his
visitor. Grabbing a pair of jeans from the dresser, he
pulled them over his hips, zipped and fastened them
and pulled on a button-down shirt, all while making
his way down the stairs to the front door where someone was now pounding away on the other side. Grasp-
ing the knob, he threw open the door.

Lucy stood with her arm raised, poised to resume
her knocking. The light spilled around her, playing
up the copper highlights in her hair.

"Hello, Lucy," Nick murmured.

"Nick."

He couldn't account for the pleasure her visit inspired. It was as if he'd been waiting all day for this
moment.

Lucy said, "I need to talk to you again."

"I can see that." He worked on fastening his buttons, needing to finish at least that much before he
let her inside.

"I have a telephone, you know," Nick said, hoping for a halfhearted apology at the very least. But he was doomed to be disappointed.

"I hate talking on the phone."

He looked at her questioningly. "Doesn't that prove difficult as a reporter?"

Irritation flashed deep in Lucy's eyes and she proudly tilted her chin. "Are you going to let me in or not?"

Nick briefly debated the merits of telling her to go away, but dismissed the idea just as quickly. If there was one thing he'd learned about Lucy, it was that she was tenacious. It was a quality that made her a top-notch reporter. Unfortunately, it didn't go well with the weary throbbing of his head.

"Fine. Come in."

Nick turned and strode into the kitchen. He had no doubt that she'd follow him.

The bang of the front door being slammed made his lips twitch in the beginnings of a smile, but he immediately wiped the humor from his expression.

"How long have you been skulking in my bushes?" He continued his lighthearted baiting as he flipped on the kitchen light.

"I have *not* been skulking in your bushes." She planted her hands on her hips. "Frankly, I've got better things to do than spy on you. I just arrived."

"Uh-huh."

He opened the refrigerator, then scowled. Other than an inch of milk left in the jug, a whole shelf of condiments and a single slice of bologna, he was out of food.

"Listen, Nick, I'd like to have you—"

"Are you hungry?" he interrupted.

Lucy gaped at him, clearly nonplussed at his inability to sense her urgency. "I haven't come to you to talk about—"

"Are you hungry?" he cut in again. "It's a simple question." Closing the refrigerator door, Nick allowed his gaze to slide down her frame, then back up again. "Because, frankly, you look like a bag of bones."

Her face froze in response. "Don't be rude," she said when she recovered from the initial shock of his words.

"I wasn't being rude. As I said the other day, you look like hell."

A glint of temper appeared in her green eyes. "I'd forgotten how ill mannered you can be."

"When was the last time you ate?"

"I had some vegetable—"

He rolled his eyes. "I'm not talking about rabbit food. I'm talking about a hot, fill-up-your-stomach meal."

Her lips pressed together in a tight line, answering that question well enough.

Nick turned away to search through the pantry closet, hoping he might find something that could be pulled together into the semblance of a meal. But it'd been so long since he'd gone to the grocery store, he knew that nothing short of a miracle could help him now.

"I didn't come here to eat." Lucy said, her tone conveying her impatience. "I came to talk to you more in-depth about the twins."

"A hotshot reporter like you can't talk and eat at the same time?"

She folded her arms tightly beneath her breasts—and for a moment, Nick was distracted.

"I don't want to eat."

Knowing now wasn't the time to be distracted, Nick dragged his eyes away from Lucy's chest. "Are you hungry or not?"

She opened her mouth and hesitated, so he took it upon himself to answer for her. "Hell, yes, you're hungry."

He brushed past her on his way to the staircase. "Wait here while I get my wallet."

"But I don't want—"

"If you want me to talk with you, you've got to eat. That's the deal."

He was midway up the stairs when he glanced down at her. From this height she looked especially thin and vulnerable.

"Agreed?"

She clenched her jaw stubbornly then finally acquiesced. "Agreed."

Chapter Three

Lucy had expected Nick to take her to an eating establishment where the menu was bolted to the wall. When they'd dated, he'd had a penchant for mom-and-pop hamburger joints, old-fashioned drive-ins and diners.

He surprised her by driving to a secluded Italian restaurant in the heart of the city. It was located in a renovated warehouse on a block populated by upscale boutiques and legal offices.

Inside, the atmosphere was quiet and sophisticated. Tables laid with heavy linen cloths were situated in intimate niches lined with potted plants. Muted murals adorned the walls and waiters wearing crisply starched shirts, black vests and ties circulated around the room.

As they stepped through the door, Lucy hung back, feeling decidedly grubby in her timeworn jeans and white button-down shirt.

"What's the matter?" Nick inquired.

"I'm not dressed for this place," she whispered.

"You look like you have plenty on to me."

"But I'm not…fancy enough."

Nick took her hand and pulled her toward the maître d'. "You're fine."

It was obvious that Nick was a regular customer. The maître d' greeted him effusively and ushered them to a table near the window. Outside, a courtyard garden had been strung with fairy lights and strategically arranged spotlights.

Lucy was entranced. She'd nearly forgotten that there were places like this in the world. Places where people could feel as if they'd stepped into a fantasy.

"Will this be all right?" the maître d' asked.

Nick glanced at Lucy and she nodded.

"Yes, thank you," he said.

When the man moved toward Lucy, Nick intercepted him to pull out Lucy's chair. Lucy couldn't remember the last time she'd been on the receiving end of such gentlemanly courtesy.

"Thanks," she murmured, sinking onto the cushioned seat and allowing him to push her closer to the table.

Nick's hand touched her shoulder, his fingers brushing against her hair as he went to his own chair.

Her mood softened even more at the gesture.

When Lucy was on assignment, she made sure her gender wasn't an issue. She carried her own equipment and stoically put up with rough conditions and the lack of privacy. Nevertheless, she couldn't deny that Nick's attentions made her feel special.

Feminine.

Alive.

As Nick settled into his place, she grabbed her menu and held it up in front of her, praying he wouldn't see the moisture that had suddenly gathered in her eyes.

Dear sweet heaven, what was wrong with her? She'd spent most of the day sleeping, so she couldn't blame her sensitivity on jet lag.

Telling herself she was just feeling stressed, she fastened her attention on the list of appetizers. Even so, she couldn't seem to control the letters that swam before her eyes.

"Everything here is good," Nick said, oblivious to her distress. "But if you order a salad, I'll personally sic the chef on you."

His comment made her snap out of her thoughts, but she couldn't afford to speak just yet. Not when her voice might emerge as a croak.

Was it a coincidence that Nick had brought her here? Or had he remembered that Italian food was one of her weaknesses? She loved everything about it—the intoxicating aromas, the combination of spices, the rich sauces, the fresh meats and cheeses.

"Well, what do you think?"

Quickly blinking the last vestiges of tears from her eyes, Lucy focused on her menu. After reading only the first few items, she expelled a sigh of pleasure. "I have died and gone to heaven," she said under her breath. At that moment, she vowed to stop worrying about the man who sat across from her, the appropriateness of her attire, or her unusual sensitivity. Her only concern would be which delectable concoction she'd taste first.

"If you look near the bottom of the menu, you'll see they have a sampler of some of the most popular dishes."

Lucy's stomach growled in anticipation.

"There's also soup, a side salad with a house dressing, bread sticks…. Just make sure you leave room for dessert."

"Dessert?" she breathed, her eyes already scanning the list on the back cover.

"They have a raspberry lemon cheesecake that will make you weep."

As if you aren't on the verge of tears already.

By the time the waiter returned to take their orders, Lucy had managed to whittle her choices down to a somewhat manageable size. In the end, she chose a sampler of lasagna with red-pepper noodles, spinach and walnut ravioli in a white sauce and chicken picatta.

Once the waiter settled a tureen of minestrone soup and a basket of fresh bread in front of them, Lucy eagerly began filling their bowls.

"So when *was* the last time you had a decent sit-down meal?" Nick asked as she began smoothing herb butter on her bread.

Lucy shrugged. "It depends on your definition of 'sit-down.' It's been at least a year since I've had Italian."

"A lifetime, then, considering your love of Italian food."

So he *had* remembered.

"Tell me about the twins."

To her shame, Lucy realized that she had momentarily forgotten about the babies who were en route to Salt Lake City.

Wrenching her brain away from the way the subtle lighting seemed to caress the angular lines of Nick's features and bring back to her responsibilities, she asked, "What would you like to know?"

"I suppose you'd better start at the beginning. How did you become their guardian?"

She took her time answering, swallowing a spoonful of soup before saying, "I was reporting on the humanitarian conditions in the war-torn regions of the Congo in Zaire, and I did a series on the orphanages in the area. I'd only been there a week when an orphanage run by a group of Franciscan nuns contacted me. At the time, the twins were just a few days old. Their mother had died in childbirth and the nuns feared that their own meager medical facilities were inadequate for the situation. They were hoping that, with my connections, I could help arrange for the girls' care in the United States."

"Yet it's taken weeks to get them here. What kind of attention have they had in the meantime?"

Her forehead creased as familiar concerns pushed to the fore. "They were transferred immediately to a larger hospital, but it's taken that long to process the reams of paperwork. I have copies of their medical files for you, but other than simple X rays, they haven't had any tests to determine if they can be separated. The hospital was more worried about getting the children stabilized. The twins were losing weight and having trouble maintaining their temperature. At one point, Hope, the smaller girl, caught an infection, which set them back a bit."

"What exactly do you know about conjoined twins?"

Lucy paused, then set down her spoon. Resting her arms on the table, she clasped her fingers together. "To be honest, the research I've done has been far from reassuring."

"Why is that?"

Reluctantly, she met his gaze, knowing that she wouldn't be able to mask her fears.

"Since my resources were somewhat limited, I was forced to get most of my information from the Internet. With some searching, I was able to find some medical texts, but first I had to wade through page after page of historically dated, sensationalist garbage. The most disturbing are the references to so-called Siamese twins being used in circus sideshows or being kept hidden from *polite society.*"

"It upsets you."

"Yes, it upsets me. Faith and Hope are *children,* not oddities to be ogled or dismissed." She took a deep breath. "And yet, if it weren't for the nuns, they could have been trapped in a similar situation."

"So you're intent on a separation?"

"Only if it's in the twins' best interests."

"And if it isn't?" he asked carefully, knowing there were be no guarantees that such an operation would be successful.

"Then I can accept that prognosis. I would like them to have healthy and productive lives, whether that means as separate individuals or not. But no matter what happens, I intend to make sure they're given the dignity and respect that every human being deserves."

Nick nodded. "And what will happen to them after you've done as much as you can?"

The words were spoken with great care, as if he expected a heated reply.

Lucy sighed, leaning back in her chair. "Because of the death of their mother, the sisters arranged for me to become the girls' legal guardian. If—no, *when* their condition is stable—I've been assigned the task of finding suitable adoptive parents for them. I've taken a six-month leave of absence from work…"

The waiter appeared to take away their empty soup bowls, interrupting Lucy. It was evident from the way she'd spoken that Lucy was anticipating a time when the twins would be healthy individuals, but Nick was relieved that she realized a completely positive outcome might be unattainable.

Yet he was well aware that totally preparing one-self for the realities of such a serious operation was not entirely possible. There were so many obstacles that lay in the children's paths—the least of which was whether or not they could tolerate the surgery. If the option proved feasible, the process of preparation and recuperation from the invasive procedure could take months, even years.

What would happen in that time? Lucy had said she intended to find adoptive parents for the babies—but what if the children grew attached to *her*? Since their own mother had died in childbirth, it was Lucy who'd been the most constant influence in their lives.

The waiter finally stepped away, leaving each of them a small dish of gelato to clear their palates after the soup course.

"Tell me more about the twins themselves," Nick prompted.

He watched with rapt attention as Lucy began to tell him about "her girls." As she regaled him with stories of their distinct personalities and physical development, he was struck by how…*maternal* she sounded. It was a side of her that was new to him. Lucy had always focused single-mindedly on her career. She ate, drank, slept and breathed reporting. Long before she'd left him, she'd made it clear that children weren't part of her plans for years to come—if ever.

Yet, since her return, he couldn't honestly remember Lucy talking about her work. Any mention of her reporting at all had been in connection with the children. It was as if she'd turned off her professional drive for the time being.

Although Nick found this unexpected parental

facet of her personality intriguing, it merely added
to his worries. Chances were strong that Lucy would
have to return to her job at CNC before the twins
were fully recovered and ready to be adopted. The
children were bound to be affected by her disappear-
ance from their lives.

But although he felt some misgivings, Nick didn't
voice them. Now wasn't the moment. After all, it had
been Lucy's job and the demands on her time and
safety that had been the major hurdle in their relationship years ago. As for now…

It was none of his business how Lucy led her life
or conducted her affairs. His only concern was the
children and how best to care for them.

LUCY SETTLED ONTO the smooth leather seat of
Nick's Mercedes, deliciously sated. She couldn't remember the last time she'd eaten such a wonderful
dinner. Years, probably.

Leaning her head back, she closed her eyes. In her
lap, she held a container with enough leftovers for a
whole meal, perhaps two.

"When does the plane land?"

"Eleven." A glance at the dashboard confirmed
that they had more than ninety minutes before pick-
ing up the twins. First, they'd stop at Nick's house
and exchange his car for the van she had leased ear-

lier that afternoon. Then they'd return to the Salt Lake International terminal where the children and their nurses would be processed through customs.

Lucy could barely contain her excitement. All her carefully made plans were about to be set in motion. After suffering through the overwhelming amount of red tape involved in bringing the children to the United States, she'd mentally prepared herself for the worst, knowing that at any moment a technicality could delay the situation yet again. But the plane had safely left Chicago and would begin its descent within the hour.

Lucy yawned as the Mercedes slowed. Realizing that she'd fall asleep if she allowed herself to get any more relaxed, she straightened.

"You've gone to a lot of trouble on behalf of the twins," Nick said as they pulled in to the driveway and rolled to a stop.

Lucy shrugged. "I never really thought of it that way. I've done what needed to be done."

He turned, his arm resting on the back of her seat. One of his fingers toyed idly with a lock of her hair.

"Why have you gone to all this effort? You aren't related to the children and there are other relief agencies who could have assumed the responsibility of getting them medical care."

His question pricked her heart. "Do you think so

little of me that you'd expect me to turn my back on someone in need?"

He grimaced. "I didn't mean to imply that I felt you were callous. I simply…" He sighed, his hand moving to the back of her head and resting there. "You've always been so driven by your career. Yet now, you're willing to step away from it all for a pair of strangers. It's a side of you I've never experienced before."

She pulled away from him. "You must have thought I was really shallow."

Tugging at the latch, she escaped from the car and strode toward the van. But she'd only taken a few steps before Nick caught her.

"Again, you've misunderstood." With his hands on her shoulders, he drew her toward him. "I'm impressed by the fact that you've put your life on hold. I'm impressed by your dedication in tackling the hundreds of details it's taken to bring them here. When we were engaged, I concentrated so intently on the passion of our relationship that I didn't appreciate your giving nature until you were gone."

The admission stunned her. He'd missed her? Even more shocking was his willingness to admit it.

Nick drew her closer, and Lucy didn't have the will to resist. She pushed away the sensible part of her consciousness that warned her an embrace could only lead to trouble. Instead, she surrendered to the heat that flooded her body.

It had been so long since she'd felt this way. So very long.

When his lips touched hers, she rested against him, her hands absorbing the solid warmth of his chest through the soft texture of his shirt. Then she rose on tiptoe, drowning in the heady desire that Nick's kiss created.

"Even when you're a sack of bones, you're the most beautiful woman I've ever known," he murmured when he pulled back to trail his lips from her cheek to her jaw, then down the sensitive arch of her neck.

"Flatterer," she breathed, the sarcasm of her remark lost in the barely audible response.

She curled her fingers into his hair, drawing him up for another kiss. Yet, even as the passion raced through her, she wasn't foolish enough to think any good would come from this moment. She was playing with fire and she would be burned. It was inevitable.

It was also the first time in years that she'd felt thoroughly alive….

But as much as she wanted to revel in the emotions she was feeling, Lucy knew she couldn't. So much depended on her. She couldn't allow herself to be sidetracked—especially not for selfish reasons.

Dragging her lips away, she whispered, "We need to go."

"Okay."

"Right now."

He took a deep breath, nodded, then finally released her. "Fine. We'll go. Right now."

LUCY HAD THOUGHT that Nick would want to bring his own car so he could return directly home from the airport. But he seemed in no hurry, saying he'd come with her in the van, then take a cab from her hotel.

They arrived at Salt Lake International well before eleven o'clock and stowed the van in the short-term parking lot. Then they made their way to the appropriate terminal, where they began their wait.

From the outset, Lucy couldn't stay still. She paced back and forth between the ticket counters and the baggage claim area, causing more than one security officer to eye her carefully.

Finally, Nick grabbed her wrist. "If you don't calm down, you're going to attract security's attention."

"Sorry."

"They'll be here soon enough, and from that point on you'll be running nonstop. You should enjoy your last few moments of solitude."

"You make it sound like I'm an expectant mother."

He looked at her inquiringly. "Aren't you?"

His words made her pause, but she shook her head. "I'm only one person in a team of caretakers."

"And how is that different from a mother who relies on the help of nannies, family or day care to help with her children?"

"My role is temporary."

He frowned. "Not to those little girls. Right now, you are the most stable influence in their lives. You're their protector and their cheerleader—and they're going to need one hundred percent of your commitment." His eyes softened. "Something I think they already have."

Warmth rose in her cheeks. Sometimes, she was sure her "commitment" bordered on an obsession. The moment she'd first held the children and felt their tiny bodies moving against her she'd known she could never let them down.

"Miss?"

She turned when a skycap approached.

"Are you Lucy Devon?"

"Yes."

"I thought I recognized you from TV," he said with smile. "I was asked to tell you that the party you're waiting for has arrived safely and the children are well. They will be down as soon as they clear customs." He held up a set of luggage tickets. "I'll gather these and meet you by the baggage claim area."

Lucy took Nick's hand, urging him toward the base of the escalator where a group of people had gathered to welcome arriving passengers.

Within minutes, two dark-skinned women appeared on the landing. One pushed an oversize carriage-type stroller, while the other carried a large diaper bag and wheeled a small suitcase.

"It's them. It's them!" Lucy waved, bouncing up and down. Impulsively, she squeezed Nick's arm, then ran toward the elevator.

At the sight of her, the weary women broke into smiles and called out.

"Lucy!"

"Hello!"

Nick remained behind, watching as the pair maneuvered the stroller and their belongings onto the elevator. As the car made its short trip to the lower level, they peered impatiently through the glass walls.

Finally, the doors slid open and they stepped out.

"Tamika, Kyro! Welcome!" Lucy hugged the two nurses, then bent to peer into the buggy. "Hello, sweet things," she cooed. Her hand disappeared as she caressed the children, then she turned to the nurses again. "Any problems?"

"No, ma'am." Tamika's voice held a hint of her native dialect mixed with a clipped British intonation. "They slept most of the way." Her lips twitched in a little smile. "Kyro was not so fortunate."

Kyro's cheeks took on a rosy hue. "I did not like—" she searched for the right words "—the height."

Lucy offered her another hug. "Don't worry, Kyro. No more flying for quite some time. I promise."

Looking at Nick, Lucy gestured for him to come closer. "This is Dr. Nick Hammond. Nick, I would like you to meet Tamika and Kyro Tabumba. They're recently graduated nurses who've been caring for the twins since their birth. And they're sisters, as I'm sure you've already guessed. They agreed to accompany the children and serve as their nannies for a few months."

The women shyly held out their hands and Nick shook them, nodding slightly. "It's a pleasure to meet you."

The women's smiles grew wide.

"Would you like to be introduced to the twins?" Lucy asked.

"Of course."

Lucy drew him forward until he could see two infants lying face-to-face. They wore frilly bonnets and were wrapped in a puffy quilt edged in candy-pink ruffles.

"May I?" Nick asked, indicating the blanket.

"Yes."

He gently pulled the quilt down to reveal two tiny bodies in pink pajamas.

Even knowing exactly what he would find, Nick's first full glimpse of the children was shocking. Great care had been taken to sew their outfits together, and the drape of the fabric hid much of what lay beneath, but it was still obvious that the children were fused from sternum to abdomen.

Automatically, Nick's training took over as he made a quick examination. He was pleased to see that—although they had feeding tubes and their bodies seemed quite small for their age—the girls appeared stable and strong.

"They look like fighters," he murmured, replacing the blanket.

"Yes, they are," Lucy agreed proudly. "They've gone through so much to make it this far."

"Shall we go get the luggage?"

Nick relieved the nurses of their carry-on bags while Lucy took control of the stroller. As the women marched ahead of him, Nick had to remind himself that he hadn't formally committed himself to helping the twins. But as he followed in the wake of these three determined women, he knew it would be futile to resist. Not only would he have Lucy and the nurses to contend with if he refused…

But he'd have to explain himself to a pair of twins who had already wriggled their way beneath his professional detachment.

Chapter Four

As soon as they reached the van, the women turned their attention toward removing the children's carrier from the stroller tray and buckling it into the backseat while Nick and the skycap loaded the luggage in the rear. They were so involved in their task and in catching up on events that Nick managed to smoothly take the car keys from Lucy and slip into the driver's seat, uncontested.

The ride through the darkened streets to downtown Salt Lake City took only a few minutes. At Lucy's request, he made his way to the Grand Hotel and maneuvered into one of the parking spaces in the underground lot.

Although Nick had devoted his career to children, he'd never quite realized how much...stuff they required. Granted, the twins had arrived with all their worldly goods, but...

Good Lord. After seeing the women and children safely to a pair of adjoining rooms, Nick needed two more trips to gather the suitcases, bags and stroller, as well as a case of formula and another of diapers. He could have arranged for a bellboy, he supposed, but when the women gathered around the babies, he'd felt like an interloper. He'd wanted to give them a few minutes alone.

As he slung two more bags over his shoulders and toted the case of formula, Nick's forehead creased in a frown. Regardless of the fact that the twins were being sponsored by an international children's aid society, he couldn't imagine that such largesse would extend to a long stay in a hotel for all five of them. Nor could he imagine that Lucy's salary—whatever it might be—could stretch to accommodate such an extravagance. Lucy might have taken his help for granted, but he doubted that she would've looked for a place to live until she was sure the twins would be staying in Salt Lake.

Hitting the up button with his elbow, he stepped into the elevator, watching the blinking lights that signaled his progress to the sixth floor. Then, moving into the hall, he made his way to the hotel room and tapped the door with his foot.

Immediately, Lucy swung the door open.

"Is that everything?"

Nick nodded. "That's it."

He set the items down, but before Lucy could return to the couch where the nurses were playing with the girls, he hooked her elbow and pulled her aside.

Gesturing to the cramped quarters, he said, "A hotel might not be the best place for the children right now."

He wasn't sure that Lucy had even heard him. She was smiling at the twins as they reached for a string of beads that Kyro held above their heads.

"It's a temporary situation," she said absently. "I've already begun searching for a furnished apartment closer to the hospital."

Although her plan was logical, Nick frowned again. The little girls deserved better than to stay in this crowded space. They deserved…

A real home with spacious rooms and cozy furniture.

The second that thought surfaced, Nick pushed it away. He had to remember that he was the children's doctor, nothing more. He had no right to make any decisions other than those that directly affected their medical condition.

"Would you like to join us for a snack?" Lucy asked. "We were just about to send for room service."

Again, Nick got the distinct impression of being

an intruder. Although Lucy had come to him for help, he reminded himself that he had no role in this unique situation other than a professional one. And he of all people should know that, as a physician, he needed to keep a measure of emotional detachment.

"I've got to go," he said abruptly, deciding that he'd wait to perform a proper examination of the children in his office. He'd seen enough to know they were primarily healthy and doing reasonably well on their own.

Lucy spun around, clearly taken by surprise, but he didn't bother to offer an explanation.

"I'll call you as soon as I've made appointments for the twins."

She opened her mouth to object, but Nick didn't give her a chance. He set the van keys on the case of formula, then walked out the door and strode down the carpeted hallway to the stairwell, desperately needing a burst of physical activity to release the tight knot of tension that was forming in the pit of his belly.

After taking the six flights with the speed of a man being pursued, he hailed a cab, then let himself into his house without remembering how he'd come to be there.

Pocketing his keys, he crossed to the staircase that led to his bedroom. But when his hand touched the newel post, he paused, suddenly struck by the silence of his home.

From the moment the twins had arrived, he'd been surrounded with a symphony of sound—the cooing of the children, the singsong melody of the women who talked to them and the tinkle of baby toys. But here in his own home there was nothing to disturb the silence.

Nick had always considered himself fortunate. He had a fulfilling career and enough money for whatever luxuries he wanted. He was a law unto himself. If he wanted to order pizza three nights in a row and spend his whole weekend watching sports, he was free to do so. On those rare occasions when he'd visited colleagues who had wives and children, he'd invariably been anxious to leave, to escape the noise and chaos.

Why did tonight seem so different?

Nick gave himself a mental shake. He was tired, that was all. Tired and strangely moody—and neither were qualities with which he had any patience.

He'd make an early night of it. Perhaps he'd read part of the thriller he'd picked up but never started. By tomorrow morning, he'd be back to his old self. Of that he was sure.

LUCY WOKE with a start, dreams of a village along the Congo and the distant pounding of drums shifting into the insistent sound of knocking.

Only partially awake, she groaned and stumbled toward the hotel-room door, wondering what sort of emergency demanded her attention at…six. It was six o'clock in the morning!

Her confusion turned to irritation. Since she'd taken the nighttime feedings so Faith and Hope's nurses could get some much-needed sleep, she wasn't feeling particularly perky—or friendly—this early in the morning. By her estimation, she'd slept for less than four hours.

Peering through the peephole, she moaned again when she saw Nick on the other side. If it had been a hotel employee, she could have ignored him or complained to the management. But since Nick had promised to contact her as soon as he'd set up the appointments, she had no choice but to unlock the door and open it.

"What?" she demanded ungraciously.

Nick raised his eyebrows. "Good morning to you, too."

"It isn't officially morning until it's completely light outside."

"It *is* light outside. A fact you would have noticed if you'd opened your drapes."

He brushed past her into the room and she scowled. "I didn't open the drapes because I hadn't yet opened my eyes."

"Sorry, but I have to be at the hospital in forty-five minutes." Nick held up a paper sack. "I come bearing a peace offering."

Her nose twitched as she caught the scent of bread and noted the name of a national bagel chain stamped on the bag.

"Did you remember the cream cheese?"

"Of course."

"Then you're forgiven." She waved him toward a small table and a couple of chairs located next to the window.

"How did the twins sleep?" Nick asked.

She shrugged, taking a seat. "They were up every two hours, but that's typical for them. If one gets hungry or wakes up, the other one does as well."

"How much formula are they taking at a time?"

"Only about an ounce orally. The rest has to be given through their feeding tubes. Last night I was lucky to get them to take a half ounce. I think they've been thrown off their schedule with the traveling, and their appetite has suffered because of it."

"We'll keep an eye on them over the next couple of days."

Because Lucy was digging into the bag, it took her a moment to absorb the fact that Nick had said "*We'll* keep an eye on them."

The use of the plural struck her as odd. Did he

mean "we" in the rhetorical sense? Was he referring to the medical staff he would assemble? Or did he mean something more intimate?

When she looked up, she found him watching her carefully. She shifted uncomfortably, suddenly remembering that she was wearing little more than an oversize T-shirt.

One of the first things that Lucy had been forced to abandon after becoming a part of the elite CNC foreign correspondents corps was her sense of self-consciousness. Often, she'd lived in primitive conditions where she and her video crew had been forced to billet together for the duration of their stay. On such occasions, privacy was a luxury.

Tugging the hem of her shirt as close to her knees as she could, she said, "You still haven't told me why you're here."

"I have a list of appointments for the children."

"You could have used the phone for that."

"It wouldn't be nearly as much fun as taking you by surprise."

Her eyes narrowed as she searched his expression. "Should I take it this is payback for catching you unawares the last couple of evenings?"

"Only in part."

He dipped into the leather bag he'd brought with him and withdrew a sheet of yellow legal paper folded in half. He slid it across the table, but when she reached for it, he drew it back again.

"Not so fast." His eyes had become dark, nearly black. "If I'm going to work on this case, I think we'd better set some ground rules."

Rules? What could he possibly mean?

"I think we both agree that the children's welfare is our primary concern," he continued.

Why did she have the sudden feeling that a trap was being set for her? "Yes, of course."

"And our past association has no bearing whatsoever on the present."

"Agreed."

"Good. But before we go any further, I need clarification on how you came to be the children's guardian."

"Of course." Lucy paused, wondering how she could condense three months' worth of government red tape into as few words as possible.

"When the children's mother died and the twins were left at the orphanage, they automatically became wards of the orphanage and the government of Zaire. Almost instantly, the nuns began investigating the possibility of bringing the girls to the United States for medical attention. Knowing that the children would need continued care, they petitioned the government for permission to have the children adopted in the U.S., even though prospective parents hadn't been found yet. Under the agreement, the children would be relinquished into the custody of a temporary legal guardian, preferably an American citizen."

"You."

"Yes. In agreeing to become the children's temporary legal guardian, I signed papers in which I promised to safeguard the children's interests in the same way a birth parent would. In addition, as far as the children's health permits, I agreed to arrange to relinquish my guardianship to a permanent adoptive family within the space of a year. If I haven't found a suitable situation in that time, then the government of Zaire reserves the right to appoint its own guardian and review all of the arrangements."

"It all sounds complicated."

"Very. And to be honest, the government officials I worked with in Zaire were bending the rules about as far as they could. Normally, arranging for an adoptive child to be brought back to the United States could take years."

"So, in essence, you have all the rights and powers of a birth parent?"

She nodded. "Yes—something I'm sure would never have been granted if not for my so-called celebrity status and the fact that one of the government officials had worked with me on a piece concerning the plight of refugees emigrating from Zaire."

"But your legal role as the twins' guardian will only last a year?"

"At that time my role would be reviewed. Of course, I intend to do everything possible to see that adoption proceedings begin before then. I brought all the necessary documentation required to make a final adoption legal from Zaire's standpoint. Nevertheless, even with my status as the children's guardian, I plan to stay in contact with the nuns and the government officials who placed so much trust in me."

"Naturally." Nick cleared his throat. "Okay, Lucy, then I think you'll concur that, when it comes to matters concerning their physical welfare, my word is paramount."

Lucy was obviously taken aback. "I would never have pegged you as a surgeon with an ego."

"It's not a matter of my ego. It's necessity. Whatever happens, the twins' care will be our complete focus in the next few months. There can be only one boss on the project, and that's me. You, on the other hand, are the parent, as far as this situation is concerned. I will offer you all the information you'll need to make whatever choices might arise. But once you've made your decisions, you need to trust me to do whatever I think is necessary to give these girls the fighting chance they deserve."

"Yes, of course."

"Then I have one more demand before I take the job."

Lucy felt a prickling at the base of her neck, sensing that she wouldn't like what he was about to say.

Nick removed a key from the pocket of his shirt. Setting it on top of the yellow paper, he slid both toward her.

"I did a great deal of thinking last night. Generally, in cases of conjoined twins, the work is done pro bono."

Lucy dismissed him with a wave of her hand. "The financial arrangements have been made. The twins' bills are being paid."

"Yes, I'm aware of that. But you didn't let me finish." His finger tapped the paper. "In the past, when we've worked with conjoined twins, arrangements were made by the hospital and local charitable institutions to provide living arrangements for the children and their parents."

"But I've been looking for an apartment."

"Hear me out. I came to the conclusion last night that one of the most important aspects in caring for the children will be my ability to keep a close eye on their progress. Added to that is the possibility that they may need special equipment before and after their surgery. A cramped rental apartment may not be the best solution."

A niggling suspicion began to bloom in her chest. Her body grew hot, then cold.

"I think it would be best for everyone involved if you, the nannies and the children moved into my house for the duration of their stay."

"I hardly think that's necessary," Lucy said quickly. She was having a hard enough time keeping her equilibrium during their visits; she could only imagine the state of her nerves if she was living with him full-time.

"I think it's very necessary. And unless you agree to that stipulation, I won't take on this case."

"That's blackmail!"

"No, it's a safe, convenient plan made with the children's welfare as a priority."

"We both know that I could find a place that would be equally safe."

"But not as convenient for me."

Her lips thinned, then she slowly said, "Somehow, I have the feeling that more is at stake in the arrangement than the twins' welfare. Am I correct in assuming that your reasons might have a personal element as well?"

His eyes narrowed, but he merely said, "Take it or leave it."

Lucy wanted to refuse, to insist that those measures weren't necessary—and to claim that any other physician wouldn't have made such a stipulation. But one look at Nick's set features convinced her that there was no point in arguing. He wouldn't change his mind. Nick could be very, very stubborn.

Lucy took a deep breath, knowing that she had no real choice. As much as she dreaded the thought of living in the same house as Nick, she couldn't allow her own misgivings to interfere with the children's needs. She'd made a vow to the nuns, herself and the twins that she'd see this through to the end. Come hell or high water, she would ensure that Faith and Hope received the best treatment available.

And the best surgeon for the job was Nick Hammond.

"All right." The words fell from her lips without her having consciously formed them, but she forced herself to say the rest. "When would you like us to move in?"

FROM THE MOMENT Lucy stepped into Nick's home carrying an armload of luggage, she felt as if the little control she possessed over her current situation began slipping from her fingers.

Ten minutes after her arrival, the deliveries began—groceries, bottled water, even a diaper service. There were extra recliners for the living room, towels and toiletries for the bathrooms and comfortable lounge chairs for the pool area to augment the simple picnic table and chairs.

Kyro and Tamika chattered on and on about how generous the doctor was being, how thoughtful. But Lucy couldn't help feeling irritated by his show of wealth. She had tried to provide for the twins as best she could, but it was obvious that she'd never have been able to supply half the amenities that were offered in Nick's home.

So with each ring of the doorbell, she grew more tense and her irritation toward the man built. Therefore, it was with genuine relief that she buckled in the children and headed to town for the first of many appointments that would begin the diagnostic process.

Although the children had arrived with X rays and several thick folders filled with information about their medical background, Nick and the other specialists were intent on gathering their own data and verifying everything that had already been determined.

Lucy was grateful for their thoroughness. Although she'd had no complaints about the way the girls had been treated to this point, she appreciated the fact that nothing would be taken for granted. The twins would be examined, tested and retested until the professionals involved had enough information to make a judgement about the feasibility of a separation.

Yet Lucy quickly learned that the testing itself wasn't the hardest part of the experience. The hardest part was having to wait for long stretches at a time, filling out countless forms and trying to keep two jet-lagged little girls happy, fed and entertained through a process that must have been frightening and sometimes painful. Under normal circumstances, she would have had Kyro and Tamika help, but they'd been so tired after their journey she'd given them the day off.

"How's it going?"

Lucy started at the sound of the deep voice and glanced up from yet another form.

Her heart fluttered in her chest when she saw Nick. She'd been told several times that he was in surgery and wouldn't meet with her until after the tests had been completed. She'd relied heavily on that information to keep her nerves on an even keel. But now, unexpectedly, he'd appeared at her side.

Lucy felt her cheeks grow hot. Faith was snuffling piteously after having just had blood taken from her heel, and Hope was crying. Since the social worker assigned to their case had insisted she needed the papers immediately, Lucy had been trying to write with one hand and lightly bounce the stroller with the other.

"Things are fine, just fine," Lucy said breezily.

"Liar."

Without asking her permission, Nick reached into the buggy and scooped the girls into his arms. "Go ahead. Finish what you were doing."

Nick settled into one of the low, stuffed chairs nearby.

"Hello, ladies," he cooed, stroking one girl's head, and then the other's. Immediately, their complaining ceased and they blinked at him with wide brown eyes. "How has your day been so far, hmm?"

Lucy could not have looked away had her hair been on fire. She'd always been a sucker for a display of gentleness—and there was nothing more attractive than a man who was comfortable with babies. But the rapport Nick had with the children went beyond mere comfort. He obviously loved being with them. His tone, his manner, his rapt expression all clearly conveyed that he welcomed the chance to play.

So why wasn't he married? He'd be a great dad.

Annoyed with the direction her thoughts were taking, Lucy forced her attention back to the forms. But she found it impossible to concentrate, and all too soon, she was peering at Nick again.

"Have you had enough to eat today, my little princesses?"

He was speaking to them softly, making exaggerated faces that obviously delighted Faith and Hope.

"Could I convince you to eat a little more? You don't want to keep those nasty tubes in your noses, do you? They really aren't the fashion this year."

He rested the girls against his chest, took their bottles and held both of them in place for the infants. The girls began to suck without any coaxing at all.

"You have a way with them." The words slipped from Lucy's mouth before she could stop them, and she could've kicked herself.

"Nah. Babies are naturally drawn to a male voice."

Lucy could have pointed out that many men had been in contact with the children throughout the day and none of them had come close to inspiring the open delight that Lucy had just witnessed.

"I'm surprised you don't have any of your own, Nick."

Damn. Why couldn't she learn to hold her tongue?

"I've never had time for a family."

At least that was one thing he wouldn't blame on their broken relationship.

"I guess having been burned once, I've never been willing to consider marriage a second time."

Maybe he *did* blame her, after all.

"What about you, Lucy? Have you changed your mind about having a family?"

"No, I haven't." She began writing furiously on the forms, hoping she was providing coherent information and not gibberish.

"Do I detect a defensive note?"

"Not at all. Like you, I've simply been too busy to consider having children."

"And if you weren't so busy, would you consider it?"

What an odd question.

"I don't know what you mean."

"I just wondered if you're at all concerned about the ticking of your biological clock or if you've decided against having babies altogether."

Her fingers gripped the pen so tightly that she feared it would snap.

"Is that a crack about my age?"

Nick laughed. "No. I'm merely asking if you'd ever consider becoming a mother."

She swiveled to face him completely. "Frankly, although it's none of your business, I have considered motherhood."

Liar.

"But now isn't the right time."

Thankfully, he didn't press her as to when she expected the "right time" to be.

During the exchange, the babies had fallen asleep. Setting the bottles in the pram, Nick patted the girls' backs, obviously an old pro at matters like burping. Lucy, on the other hand, had needed some coaching by the nuns before she'd realized the full importance of this practice.

"How long before you can decide about an operation?"

Nick made a tsking sound. "Patience, patience. There are a million steps we'll have to take before we know if it's even possible. We're on number…five." His eyes creased at the corners as he smiled. "The girls are stable and growing. Right now, their biggest concerns are jet lag and removing the feeding tube. Just concentrate on those for now."

Resolutely, Lucy turned back to the papers in front of her. She purposely kept her gaze away from Nick, even when she heard a pair of muffled burps and a rustling as Nick settled the twins back into their stroller.

But when he moved toward her and laid his hand on Lucy's shoulder, she couldn't still the tremor that raced through her body.

"Relax, Lucy. They'll be fine."

Then, as she sat there shaking with a mixture of awareness and nerves, he left her just as suddenly as he'd come.

Chapter Five

By seven o'clock in the evening when Lucy pulled the van into Nick's driveway, she was exhausted and her head throbbed.

As she maneuvered the vehicle into the space next to the garage, the kitchen door opened and the two nurses bounded outside, their faces wreathed in smiles.

"Hello!"

"Hello!"

They slid open the large passenger door and peered inside at their charges.

"Did everything go well?" Tamika asked.

"Yes, I think so. We'll know more when the doctors begin phoning with the results."

"We'll take the girls straight to bed," Kyro said as she removed the car seat. "You rest now, you hear?"

"Thank you, Kyro."

While Kyro carried the children inside and Tamika unloaded the diaper bags and baby paraphernalia, Lucy grabbed the sack of Chinese takeout she'd picked up on her way home. The house might have been stocked with groceries, but she was too proud to use Nick's food, and she hadn't had the energy to spend any time at the store.

The house was quiet when she entered. Since she didn't see Nick's keys on the hook, she surmised he was probably working late.

"Miss Lucy! Come quick!"

Panic seized Lucy's chest at Tamika's urgent cry. Dropping the bag on the counter, she hurried to the back bedroom assigned to the twins. Once in the doorway, she immediately sought out the children, but they slept peacefully in Kyro's arms, their heads resting on her chest. But as Lucy gradually took in her surroundings, her mouth gaped open in amazement.

In their absence, the bedroom had been completely transformed into a nursery complete with an overstuffed rocker, changing table and two cribs— *two*.

The edges of Lucy's lips lifted in a pleased smile—as much from the silent vote of confidence the two little beds inspired as from the quaint furnishings themselves, cheerfully decorated with bunnies and chicks. But almost as quickly, her smile disappeared.

Although she appreciated Nick's thoughtfulness, the irritation she'd felt earlier returned. The twins were *her* responsibility, but she hadn't even been consulted. What if she'd had her own ideas about the children's needs?

Even while a part of her whispered that her reaction was petty, her frustration blossomed. Such high-handed tactics were too reminiscent of the way her father had ruled her childhood home. He'd been a tyrant through and through. Invariably, he made all the decisions as to how and where their money should be spent, leaving Lucy and her mother powerless.

Don't think about that now. Don't think of him.

But Lucy couldn't help herself. From the moment she'd left home, she'd prided herself on her independence. She'd refused to ask anything of anyone. Even more important, she'd vowed that she wouldn't be ruled by a man ever again. If he couldn't meet her as an equal, then she wanted no part of a relationship.

The distant rumble of the garage door alerted Lucy to Nick's arrival. Ignoring Tamika's and Kyro's curious expressions, she turned on her heel.

When Nick walked into the kitchen, she was waiting for him. He glanced up, started to smile, then set his wallet on the kitchen counter with utmost care.

"Is something wrong?"

"You didn't tell me you'd be buying things for the twins."

Lucy realized that her statement came out sounding like an accusation.

He shrugged. "Since I was the one who insisted you stay here, I thought it would be best if I furnished the room with a few necessities."

"We won't be here that long. You've gone to a huge expense for nothing."

He rested a hand on the counter, shifting his weight to one foot. Despite his attempt at casualness, his body gave the impression of being ready for an attack if necessary.

"Perhaps. But it could also be several months after their surgery before they're ready to travel. Don't you think they deserve to be comfortable?"

"That isn't the point."

"Then what is?"

She folded her arms across her chest. "*I* am the children's guardian. I may have given you temporary power over decisions regarding their medical treatment, but that's where your role in their lives ends."

The silence that followed was thick with tension.

"I'm sorry if you interpreted my actions as anything other than helpful. I merely wanted to give the children and their nannies a comfortable, stimulating environment. Heaven only knows that Faith and Hope will be frightened by unfamiliar faces, sterile hospital rooms and painful procedures. In light of all that, I thought buying a couple of cribs was the least I could do."

Lucy flushed, suddenly ashamed of her outburst. Nick was right, damn him.

Nick reached out and caressed her cheek.

"Is it just the furniture that has you in knots or is there something more?"

Damn him again. She'd forgotten how easily Nick had been able to read her. Generally, she was capable of keeping her thoughts and emotions hidden. But Nick had an uncanny ability to see through her mask every time.

"I just don't like having decisions taken out of my hands."

He nodded curtly. "You're right. I'm sorry. I should have consulted with you."

"I'll pay you back."

"No. You won't. When I suggested that you stay here, I had every intention of footing the expenses."

"Absolutely not! I'll pay you the same amount I would've paid for rent, and I insist on buying all the food."

He shook his head. "I may not know exactly how much a foreign correspondent makes, but I do know that the expenses the children will incur over the next few months will be enormous."

She bristled with pride. "I've already found financial backing to—"

"I know, and I commend you for seeing to that. But as I said before, in cases such as these, doctors and nurses often volunteer their services to keep costs to a minimum. It makes us feel good to know we're helping those who don't have the means to help themselves. I will not let you stand in the way of my personal contribution."

When he put it like that, her position seemed petty, but she couldn't resist saying, "You're already doing more than enough. I have to pay rent at the very least."

"Why? Why can't you simply accept a gift that's being offered to you?"

Because Lucy had learned long ago that "gifts" were rarely free. One way or another, a price would have to be paid.

But she didn't say the words aloud. Instead, she carefully backed away from him, realizing that if she didn't leave now, she would either argue with him more or…

Or succumb to the desire that was already beginning to twine around her like an ensnaring vine.

"Thank you for your thoughtfulness on behalf of the girls," she whispered. Then, knowing her control could only stretch so far, she left the room.

As he watched her go, Nick wondered what nerve he'd hit in decorating the girls' room. Lucy's reaction had been due to more than mere pride. There had been a note of...*fear* in her voice.

But fear of what?

His interference?

Or something within herself?

Lucy had always been guarded with her emotions. Nick had attributed it to shyness when they'd first met, but after several months of dating, he'd known he was dealing with more than just natural reticence.

Sighing, Nick followed his nose to the bag on the counter. But even as he discovered a treasure trove of Chinese food, his mind kept veering to the woman who had stormed from the room.

He was beginning to see that marrying Lucy so long ago would have been a horrible mistake—not because of who she was but because they hadn't really known each other. Rather than communicating, they'd pushed aside their concerns, sure that they'd have plenty of time to "work things through."

Even though they'd been engaged, there was so much Nick didn't know about Lucy Devon. He was consumed with the need to discover why she was so afraid of her own emotions. He wondered if even she knew the answer.

Leaving the food untouched, he made his way to the back bedrooms. Seeing that Kyro and Tamika were alone with the girls in the nursery, he kept walking until he noticed that Lucy's door was slightly ajar.

"Lucy," he began with a cursory tap that pushed the door open farther.

She gasped, whirling to face him, her shirt partially unbuttoned.

"Will you knock, please?" she demanded.

"I did knock."

"Then wait for an answer."

"Touché."

She scrambled to refasten her blouse. "What do you want?"

Nick was too taken by the sight of her exposed skin to answer at first, but he finally forced himself to say, "I came to tell you that you were right, I've been very dictatorial about this whole affair."

Her eyebrows rose in obvious surprise. "Oh, really."

"Yes, really."

"So you'll let me pay rent?"

"No."

She scowled.

"But I'll let you feed me three times a week."

She stared at him, then said, "You found the Chinese food."

His lips twitched. "It smells great."

"I'd hardly call a few meals a compromise."

"Look. It's ridiculous to pay me rent, when I own the house and these rooms would just be going empty. The furniture can either be kept for the next needy case we encounter or it can be auctioned for charity. Either way, it's a tax write-off for me. So three meals is fair."

"All of them."

"Three meals."

"Three meals, a couple of breakfasts and Tamika's famous sweet bread," she countered.

He nodded. "Agreed."

She smiled in open satisfaction at having "bested" him, and he didn't correct her on the assumption. For the moment, he would have given anything to see her wide, uninhibited smile.

"I'll meet you in ten minutes for chicken balls and lo mein," he said, pushing away from the door.

"Make it fifteen."

She was still arguing. But for the moment, he didn't care.

"Fine. Fifteen it is."

IN THE DAYS that followed, Lucy doted on the children, showering them with toys and new clothes—until even she was forced to admit that her purchases were getting out of hand. She had planned long ago to wait until she arrived in the United States to augment the girls' wardrobes and supplies. But once she began shopping, Lucy didn't seem to be able to stop. Much like the "other parent" in a custody battle, Lucy found herself competing with Nick in order to prove her affection for the children.

Lucy was quite sure that a therapist would tell her she was overreacting to Nick's interference, but in spite of his arguments to the contrary, he *had* been extravagant in his purchases for the nursery. There was even a maid who would be coming three times a week to help with the cleaning.

Although she chided herself for behaving so immaturely, Lucy's compulsion to reassert herself as the children's main caregiver was only part of the problem. Her overindulgence had as much to do with her fear of the future as it did with her desire to show Nick that she was more than capable of providing for the girls. Time and again, she was reminded that the twins would only be with her for a short time. All too soon, Lucy would be drawn back into the career she had temporarily abandoned and the children would be adopted into a loving home.

Then Lucy would fill her life with the challenges inherent in her job.

Surprisingly, the thought of returning to work filled her with dread. Where once she had eagerly embraced killer deadlines, punishing travel schedules and constant stress, now all she wanted was to enjoy her unfamiliar, new maternal role. She'd taken a six-month leave of absence, but that suddenly seemed too brief.

Nevertheless, as much as she enjoyed playing with the children, it was something of a relief when the twins were asked to come to the hospital for more tests. She was anxious to proceed to the next step, to determine the possibility of a separation once and for all.

"They'll be fine, won't they, Miss Lucy?" Kyro asked, standing by her side at the hospital.

"Yes, I'm sure the staff will take good care of them," Lucy reassured the nurse as the children were wheeled away for their latest MRI.

"Dr. Hammond wouldn't hear of anything else," Tamika said, clasping her sister's hand.

No, Nick wouldn't accept anything but dignity and respect for his patients. The more Lucy heard about him through the other nurses and doctors, the more she knew that—despite her personal feelings—she'd done the right thing in coming to him.

Perhaps it was her own disquiet that had begun

to eat away at her belief in the twins' recovery. Lucy tried to keep her outlook positive, but with each new test and hospital visit, the task ahead of them began to seem more enormous. There were so many unknowns to uncover in the next few months. Did the girls share critical organs that could never be divided? Or worse yet, would one twin thrive at the expense of the other?

Even if the best-case scenario was possible and an operation was scheduled, that didn't mean an end to Lucy's worries. Could a separation cause future disabilities and medical challenges? Would the girls have a chance at full, happy lives, or would they be faced with debilitating health issues and perhaps even death?

At times, Lucy felt as if she was building a house of cards. Each decision she made on behalf of the children led to consequences that required new choices. Lucy could only take tiny steps forward, then wait to see if the efforts she took would withstand the inherent pressures involved.

"Do you mind if we visit the newborn babies?" Tamika inquired.

Lucy shook herself free of her own inner turmoil. "No, you two go ahead. I'll come get you once the twins are done, but it will be at least an hour."

The women eagerly headed toward the elevator

banks. Thanks to Nick's introductions, the sisters had developed a friendship with many of the nurses in the Intermediate ICU unit. Tamika and Kyro had begun to volunteer during their free time, rocking babies and helping with paperwork. Lucy knew that the opportunities they were being given would provide them with invaluable experience once they returned to Zaire.

While Lucy…

She didn't know what she'd do once the children were well.

Pacing the confines of the waiting room, Lucy tried to remind herself that she'd be better off remaining objective. But with each day that passed, she was becoming more and more attached to Faith and Hope. She had developed a fondness for them that had long since crossed the boundaries of a reporter seeking humanitarian aid.

Even though her guardianship would be fleeting, Lucy often toyed with the notion of becoming an Auntie Mame–like character in the girls' lives. One who dropped in unexpectedly from time to time, indulged them horribly, then left them to their parents to raise. And since Lucy was the person who would ultimately choose Faith and Hope's adoptive family, she didn't think it would be too difficult to find a couple who was open to such an arrangement.

So why did she feel a sense of dissatisfaction at even that magnanimous role in their lives?

The phone in her pocket bleeped and Lucy sank into one of the uncomfortable vinyl chairs.

She punched the on button. "Devon here."

"Lucy, thank God!"

She immediately recognized the shrill voice of her bureau chief's secretary and rolled her eyes. Nan Tarkington was a brusque, handsome woman prone to histrionics.

"Hello, Nan."

"Hold, please, while I connect you to Frank."

The canned music had barely begun when Frank broke in and said without preamble, "I need you in Colombia."

"Hello to you, too, Frank."

"Dammit, Lucy, I haven't got time for niceties."

"Obviously. What's happening in Colombia?"

"Three Americans have been taken hostage by local rebels."

Lucy's adrenaline started pumping. She'd been to Colombia earlier that year and a picture of the moist, dense jungle flashed in her mind. A commercial flight would take precious hours, but if she—

Her thoughts came to a screeching halt as the pristine waiting room swam into focus around her. What was wrong with her that she would even think of going? The twins were only a few yards away, so tiny and alone in a sea of unfamiliar strangers.

"I'm on a leave of absence, Frank."

"I'm well aware of that, but I need you back."

"Why?"

"The kidnappers are part of a new, radical religious group that's only surfaced in the last few months. The whole situation could blow up in a matter of weeks. I need someone experienced on-site."

"Get Kurt Rogers to go."

"He's already in Ghana."

She opened her mouth to give him a list of half a dozen other correspondents who would be itching for a chance to take the assignment, but the hair prickled at the back of her neck, warning her.

Turning, she saw that Nick had moved into the room behind her and was watching her intently. She felt an unaccountable wave of guilt.

"Frank, I can't come back yet. You'll have to find someone else."

"Dammit, Lucy! I need you. Can't you leave the kids with their nannies for a while?"

"No, Frank, I can't. Listen, I've got to go. I'm at the hospital and I'm not supposed to be using a cell phone while I'm in the building."

"But, Lucy—"

"Goodbye, Frank."

She punched the end button, then turned off the phone.

Nick eyed her with evident disapproval. "If you need to make a call, there are pay phones in the hall."

She raised her hand to stop his rebuke. "I know. I'm sorry. I forgot to turn the thing off once we got into the building. It won't happen again."

He continued to stare at her, yet she sensed that his disapproval had shifted from the use of her cell phone to the conversation he'd overheard.

"Frank is your…"

"My bureau chief. He's trying to get me to go to Colombia to follow a current crisis."

Lucy was suddenly reminded of the last time she and Nick had held a similar conversation. It had been a few days before they were to be married. A phone call from a friend had tipped Lucy about a fanatical cult in Montana that was about to be raided by the FBI. Already suffering from cold feet about her wedding, Lucy had begged Nick to postpone the ceremony for a few weeks, but he'd convinced her to continue with their plans. In the end, it had been his inability to look at her side of the argument that had made her decide to leave him. And it had been her coverage of the standoff in Montana for a local television station that had led to her job with CNC.

"Tell me, Lucy. Why are you here?" Nick asked, sliding his hands into the pockets of his lab coat.

She stiffened. "What do you mean?"

"I want to know what your motives are for helping the twins."

Lucy winced inwardly when Nick unwittingly touched a sensitive nerve. After all, hadn't she asked herself the same question more than once?

When she'd first met the girls, she'd simply wanted to find a way to help them. Lucy had always had a soft spot for children and underdogs. But in order to bring the twins to the United States, she'd been appointed their official guardian. Something about the legal formalities of the situation had changed her attitude. Instead of just being an onlooker, she'd become…a protector.

Nick continued, "I need to know, here and now, if you plan to exploit the children's situation." She gasped, but he went on as if he hadn't heard her. "If this is a publicity stunt or a way to garner ratings for CNC or any other television station, I'll pull out of this project."

"There will be no camera crews and no reporters," she said through clenched teeth.

"Do I have your word on that?"

"You don't need my word. I would never permit such a thing to happen." What she didn't say was that she'd been approached with several offers and refused.

"Then why are you here? You never really answered when I asked you earlier. What possible reason would you have to leave your career and expend so much time and energy on two little girls?"

He really thought she was heartless, didn't he? He thought her only concern was her career.

But to her shame, Lucy realized he wasn't completely wrong. Until the moment she'd first held Faith and Hope in her arms, that *had* been her only driving force. But when she'd felt the children moving against her, burrowing beneath her chin, filling her nostrils with their sweet baby scent, everything had changed. She'd become patently aware that she was alone in the world and likely to remain so. But for a few brief months, she could have something more in her life. She could *be* something more.

But how could she ever admit that to Nick? How could she explain that, every single day, the children touched her in ways she had never experienced before? She couldn't even explain the phenomenon to herself.

"Well?" Nick prodded.

"Let's just say I've been aware that my biological clock has been ticking for the past year or so—just as you'd suspected. I decided it was time to surrender to my maternal fantasies in a way that wouldn't be completely binding," she offered flippantly, praying he wouldn't hear the note of hurt that she recognized in her own voice.

Abruptly, she changed the subject. "Are the children finished for the day?"

Nick nodded and gestured to a door at the end of the hall. "The MRI is complete, but it will be a little while before they can go home. I want to make sure the sedation has worn off before you leave. In the meantime, why don't you wait in the conference room. I've got to quickly check the results of some tests on another patient. As soon as I'm done, I'll talk to you about what we've discovered so far."

"Fine."

Walking to the conference room, Lucy blinked away the moisture that gathered in her eyes. She'd known it would be difficult coming to Nick for help—and she hadn't been naive enough to think he no longer harbored any lingering resentment over the past.

Nevertheless, it hurt to realize he had such a low opinion of her that he believed she'd use the twins for her own gain.

Just as it hurt to discover how much he still had the power to wound her.

Chapter Six

Nick waited until Lucy had disappeared into the conference room before turning and making his way down the hall to the "quiet room"—a small corner-office space with computer terminals, a sleeping cot, refrigerator, hot plate and coffee machine.

He grabbed a cola from the fridge, filled a paper cup with ice and drank deeply.

It had been a hectic morning filled with rounds, teaching sessions and appointments. The rest of the day looked to be no different. He'd be lucky to get home in time for dinner.

He paused, his drink poised halfway to his lips. Now where had *that* thought come from? He was sounding a little too much like his colleagues who were eager to go home to their wives and families.

The arrangement is temporary, Nick reminded

himself as he perched on a stool in front of the computer terminal. *Don't get too attached.*

To whom?

. The children?

Or Lucy?

Forcing himself to concentrate on his work, he typed in the identification number for a six-month-old girl on whom he'd performed transplant surgery earlier that week. He checked over the bloodwork done that morning and made a note adjusting her meds. Then he stretched, his eyes drifting to the window.

When he'd emerged from studying the twins' MRI to overhear Lucy's telephone conversation, he'd been struck by an alarming sense of déjà vu. A similar phone call five years ago had begun the unraveling of their relationship. Even then, he'd known deep in his heart that the demands of her career would outweigh her feelings for him. She'd been so driven to succeed—to the point of near obsession. It was as if she'd felt it necessary to prove herself to some unknown adversary.

Sighing, Nick wondered why he couldn't put the past behind him. Since the end of his engagement to Lucy, he'd had several relationships. Six months ago, he'd even considered proposing to a fellow doctor, Maryann Goss…

Until Maryann had broken off their courtship, stating that she didn't want to compete with his past.

At the time, Nick had been furious. He'd been in-
sulted that anyone would think that he was still in
love with Lucy Devon. After all, he'd been the person wronged.

But once Nick had calmed down, he'd realized
that Maryann had been right. He was still deeply affected by his breakup with Lucy, but not for the reasons everyone thought. He wasn't hanging on to any
lingering feelings. He was just leery of putting himself into a position like that again. He didn't trust
love and he didn't trust passion. Sure, there were
people who managed to create marriages that lasted
a lifetime. But he suspected emotion had less to do
with it than sheer dogged determination.

So why couldn't he seem to remember the lessons
he'd learned? Why was he allowing himself to fall
back into the same physical intoxication he'd experienced before with Lucy? Because that was all it
was, an intoxication. An infatuation.

An addiction.

Tossing back the rest of his cola, he ignored the
growling of his stomach that reminded him he hadn't
eaten and it was nearly two in the afternoon. He
didn't have time for mundane concerns. Right now,
he needed to speak with Lucy about the twins.

As he stepped from the quiet room, he swore to
himself that he'd concentrate on business and push

everything else aside. He had to remember that Lucy wouldn't be around forever. One day soon, she would take a call like the one she'd received this afternoon, but the next time she would accept the assignment. Until then, Nick had better do his best to get her out of his system. He was tired of being haunted by memories of what might have been.

As soon as he arrived in the conference room, Nick began a detailed briefing of the twins' condition. He kept his tone curt and businesslike, focusing his attention on the results of the tests.

Through it all, Lucy watched him with an expression of overt concern that bordered on real terror— a fact that, given her wartime experiences, surprised him. Her questions were pointed and intelligent, conveying her understanding of the situation, but it wasn't until he played a tape of the most recent ultrasound that her worried frown lessened.

There, on the screen, amid the myriad dots that formed darker and lighter shapes resembling a moving Rorschach test, were two pulsing shapes.

"Those are the hearts?" Lucy breathed.

"Yes. Although their heartbeats are often synchronized, the organs are separate and distinct."

Her relief was tangible. Unconsciously, she reached out to grasp his hand with both of hers.

"Then they *can* be separated."

As much as he loved seeing her so happy, Nick knew he had to be completely honest. "We're encouraged by the fact that the girls have two separate hearts, but we're still concerned about the liver and their shared blood supply. Faith's heart seems to be larger, taking more of the burden than it should, which could pose a problem. But overall, the data we've collected looks hopeful. The other surgeons I've asked to be part of my team have agreed to continue investigating the possibility."

She laughed aloud, jumping up from her seat and throwing her arms around his neck.

The spontaneous embrace was a mistake. The moment their bodies touched, Nick was overwhelmed by memories of another time. Old passions roared to life—and judging by the sudden stillness of Lucy's body, he wasn't the only one affected.

Nick knew he was toying with disaster. He knew he should pull free from her embrace and step away. Instead, he lowered his head and their lips met, softly at first, then again and again, each time with increasing heat and abandon. His arms swept around her waist, pulling her tightly against him.

Lucy allowed desire to inundate her. Dear heaven, what was happening to her? She shouldn't want this man. Not after everything that had happened.

But as she spread her fingers over the hardness of

his chest, and the heat of his body filled every corner of her being, she knew this embrace had been inevitable. Since their last kiss the two of them had been skirting the sensual tension that filled the air around them whenever they shared the same room. She should have known she would not be able to resist him....

No. She would not give up everything she'd worked to build—her career, her reputation, her very identity—for a man. Any man.

Drawing upon every ounce of will she possessed, Lucy quickly turned away. Gulping air into her lungs, she tried to ignore the trembling of her limbs.

Close on the heels of her desire came a wave of shame and powerlessness that she remembered so well from childhood.

In an attempt to pretend that nothing out of the ordinary had happened, Lucy forced herself to ask a question about the future tests Nick had mentioned. But when he answered, she felt as if he were speaking in another language. All the while, he watched her with an all-knowing expression that stripped her vulnerability bare.

He thinks he knows me. He thinks he knows what I'm feeling, but he doesn't. He's probably gloating, sure that he's found a chink in my armor. But he's wrong.

She wasn't going to let him touch her again.

KNOWING THAT LUCY was shaken, Nick let her draw their conversation to a close and quickly leave.

Reflecting on what had just happened, Nick found his curiosity piqued even more. He noticed how Lucy had frantically tried to repair her image, once again becoming the tough, stoic reporter. It was as if she was ashamed of her momentary lapse of control.

Not for the first time, Nick wondered what had happened in Lucy's past to make her so wary of her own feelings. She seemed to be afraid of reaching out to another human being, especially in a romantic sense. Nick had had to stubbornly pursue her before she'd agreed to their first date. That ability to remain detached had served her well as a reporter, but now…

She was so alone.

It was obvious to Nick that Lucy had been right to leave him. Their relationship would never have survived. Despite the obvious conflicts with her job, it was her fear of true intimacy that would have destroyed their marriage.

And nothing had changed since then. Becoming involved with Lucy would be a stupid mistake, one he wasn't about to make again.

Nick began gathering the tapes and charts. Yet, even as his inner musings reaffirmed the importance of staying away from Lucy Devon, it took everything he possessed not to follow her and pull her back into his arms.

LUCY HAD SCARCELY LEFT the building and turned on her phone when it bleeped.

"Hello, this is Lucy Devon," she said automatically as she searched for her keys.

"Lucy, don't do that to me again!" Frank Carlisle bellowed.

She sighed, picturing her boss hunched over his messy desk, his face red, a vein throbbing in his neck.

"Calm down, Frank. You're going to have a coronary."

"Damned right I will. I've got the chance of a lifetime and I can't get you to answer the blasted phone!"

"I'm not coming back, Frank."

The silence that greeted her was ample evidence of his shock. She couldn't even count the number of times she'd canceled vacations, appointments or speaking engagements to jump on a plane for the next breaking story. Frank had come to depend on her as one of his primary troubleshooters.

"Now, Lucy…"

"You can wheedle all you like, but I can't come.

I won't come. You granted me a six-month leave of absence and I'm holding you to your word."

"I could fire you over this."

"If you do, I'll sue."

Frank sighed, clearly irritated by her response. "I'll send Erik Parker for now."

"Parker?" she echoed in disbelief. "You can't send Parker."

From the moment Erik Parker had been hired at CNC, it was obvious that he coveted Lucy's job and prestige. For the most part, she'd been able to ignore him and his underhanded efforts to manipulate Frank into offering him one plum assignment after another. But to hear Frank openly suggest him for a job that would've been hers was galling.

"Do you want to change your mind?"

She bit her lip, feeling unaccountably threatened. It wasn't as if she'd lose her job. Sure, Parker would receive some prime airtime, but when the twins were healthy, she'd be back and ready to claim her spot as one of CNC's most recognized reporters. Parker couldn't take that away from her. Not in such a short time.

"Well?" Frank prodded.

"Goodbye, Frank."

"Lucy, I—"

"Goodbye, Frank," she said firmly, then terminated the call and turned her phone off.

She realized that she'd somehow made her way to the van and stood leaning against the hood trembling.

Although Lucy knew there was nothing else she could have done, she still felt hollow. She'd never refused an assignment in her life, and she was discovering that it wasn't as easy as she would've imagined. She was so used to being in the thick of things that it was hard to accept the fact that Erik Parker would be given her assignment.

Erik Parker.

Scowling, she unlocked the car and climbed inside. Frank was more than aware of the personality clash between Lucy and Parker. Trust him to use it as a ploy to get her back.

Well, it wasn't going to work, Lucy told herself as she jabbed the key into the ignition and revved the engine. She had more important matters on her mind. The twins needed her here, not in Colombia. They—

The twins.

The twins!

Halfway out of the parking space, she jammed on the brakes and swore under her breath, just now realizing that the twins were still in the hospital waiting for her to take them home.

Lucy was overcome with embarrassment, and tears pricked at the backs of her eyes.

See? This is why you've never married or become a mother. You simply don't have what it takes to be a nurturer.

FROM HIS VANTAGE POINT by a third-floor window, Nick grinned, watching as Lucy's van eased back into the parking space.

He'd wondered how long it would take her to realize she'd forgotten the children.

Whistling to himself, he headed back toward the nurses' station. When Lucy rushed out of the building without a second glance, one of the RNs had come to ask him what was wrong.

"She's on her way back," he told her with a grin.

There wasn't any harm done; the twins would have to stay a little longer, anyway, while the sedation wore off. And Lucy wouldn't have been the first new mother who—numb with worry and lack of sleep—had momentarily lapsed into old habits. But much as he would have liked to tease Lucy about her forgetfulness, he knew he'd better avoid the temptation. He had a couple of patients to see and surgery in an hour.

Besides, it was probably in his best interests to steer clear of Lucy for a while, especially if she found out that her absentmindedness had been witnessed by most of the pediatric floor.

THE FOLLOWING AFTERNOON, Lucy left the children with their nannies and attended a meeting with the surgeons who'd been asked to serve on Nick's team. One by one, they outlined their roles, the data they planned to collect and the procedures they'd be performing if the surgery did indeed get the green light. Also in attendance were a half-dozen residents and medical students. Nick explained to Lucy that they would be observing the separation and participating in the meetings but would not take part in the actual operation.

It was evident that Nick had chosen his colleagues from the finest talent available. The men and women were capable and self-assured. But just as clear was the fact that Nick was in charge.

By the time the meeting had ended, Lucy felt as if she'd ridden an emotional roller coaster, alternating between delirious hope and paralyzing fear. She was delighted by the progress—truly, she was. But with each step her worries increased.

So much could go wrong.

After all the others had left, Nick stayed behind. He approached Lucy as she gathered her things.

"Let me take you to lunch."

His tone was gentle, nearly swaying her. But the memory of the kiss they'd shared in this same room only a day earlier bolstered her resolve. "No, I—I'm sure that you have other matters you need to attend to, and I—I should get back to the twins."

He disregarded her protests, lacing their fingers together and drawing her after him. "I know a place that has the greatest ribs you'll ever eat. Let's go there."

Mulishly, she tugged on his hand in an effort to free herself, but even she knew her protests were weak. "Don't you have appointments?"

"I thought our meeting would take much longer, so I canceled everything until midafternoon."

"But—"

He stopped, turning toward her and stroking her cheek with his finger. "Relax, Lucy. I've got my cell phone, and my receptionist has the number. I can be reached anytime there's an emergency."

Lucy knew she should argue again, but she didn't have the strength. Right now, she needed the company of someone who wasn't looking to her to make things right.

"I'm starving," she finally admitted.

"Good, because you're going to love this place."

Within twenty minutes they were sliding into vinyl-covered booth seats and perusing a pair of plastic-coated menus.

The surroundings were much more in keeping with the man Lucy had known years ago. Even Nick seemed to loosen up, ordering a cola for himself, then regarding her questioningly.

"I don't drink when I'm on call, but if you'd like wine or beer—"

"No, cola is fine."

The waitress disappeared, leaving a wooden cutting board with a small loaf of warm bread and a crock of butter.

"This is good," Lucy sighed after her first bite.

"Wait until you taste the ribs."

She smiled as she watched him quickly finish one slice and start on another. "I was beginning to believe that your success had begun to change your appetite."

Nick cocked an eyebrow.

"I've only seen you eating good-for-you food since I came here. Judging by the shape you're in, I assumed you'd sworn off red meat and ate nothing but pasta, vegetables and fruit."

"God forbid," he said with a grimace. "There's a gym in the hospital that I use to help me work off the stress. Other than that, age has been creeping up on me."

"Hardly."

"Believe me, by the end of the day I'm feeling every one of my years."

"Nevertheless, you aren't exactly ready for a retirement home."

He leaned back, having obviously eased his hunger.

"What about you? Why haven't you been taking care of yourself?"

She flinched. "I'd appreciate it if you wouldn't insist on reminding me that I... 'look like hell.'"

"Actually, you've cleaned up rather well in the past couple of days."

She shot him a pithy look.

"Why have you settled for the runway-model image?"

"I haven't 'settled' for anything. My last few assignments were to poor, underdeveloped countries, and there weren't many options available. Once I arrived in Zaire, my time was devoted to helping the twins and I never got a chance to really sit down, let alone eat a square meal."

Nick had the grace to look contrite. "I'm sorry. I should've taken all of that into account instead of just assuming..."

She gave him a small smile.

There was a beat of silence, then Nick asked, "Is it everything you'd thought it would be? Your work?"

Unspoken between them was the fact that she'd chosen her career over a life with him.

"I—"

The waitress arrived with their food, interrupting Lucy and she welcomed the distraction. For one thing, she wasn't sure how she should answer the question. Yes, she enjoyed her work. She'd met people and seen places she never would have otherwise. She'd grown as a person and as a professional.

But how could she say that to Nick without insulting him? How could she possibly explain that leaving him had been the best thing she'd ever done?

Knowing she had to keep Nick from questioning her again, she changed the subject, entertaining him with amusing stories she'd gathered over the years. They were the same anecdotes she used at parties or when she was asked to be a guest speaker—nothing too controversial or distressing.

Nick listened to her attentively, laughing and asking questions. But through it all, she suspected he hadn't completely forgotten his original question. Nor was he fooled by her glowing travelogue. He was too astute for that.

You'll have to be on your guard in the months to come, a little voice reminded her.

She couldn't afford to let him think she was anything but blissfully happy.

Chapter Seven

Once they'd finished their meal, Lucy and Nick stepped back into the sunshine. As they walked to Nick's car, Lucy tilted her head back so she could enjoy the warmth on her face.

"How are your parents, Lucy?"

She stumbled, an icy chill seeping into the pit of her stomach.

"My parents?" she echoed.

"Do they still live in the area?"

They were at the car now and she reached for the door handle. "No, I mean…my father died nearly two years ago."

"I'm sorry. I didn't know. How's your mother doing without him?"

"Oh, she's fine," Lucy said airily, the lie tainting her tongue. "She took his death hard, of course, but she's doing better."

"Does she still live nearby?"

"Hmm," she offered noncommittally, then, hearing the thump of the car's locks being released, she opened the door and slid inside.

She'd hoped that once they were in the car Nick would drop the subject, but he continued.

"Have you had a chance to visit her yet?"

Lucy felt her facial muscles tense. "No. Not yet. I thought I'd go today or tomorrow." Needing to talk about something—anything—else, she asked, "When will the children have to come back for their next set of appointments?"

Finally, she'd managed to change the subject. Yet, as Nick explained what tests would be performed the following day, Lucy had trouble concentrating.

Nick had met her parents only briefly—which was how Lucy had wanted it. She'd learned at an early age to keep friends and romantic interests away from her father. No one was ever good enough, polite enough, perfect enough to win George Devon's approval.

And her mother…

The mere thought of Lillian Devon brought a swirl of conflicting emotions—love, guilt, worry, regret.

"…all goes well, we might be able to schedule surgery within the next few weeks."

Lucy's attention wrenched back into focus. "That soon?"

"If separation is a possibility, and it looks like it is, we need to complete the surgery before any of their systems are further compromised. As I said before, Faith's heart seems to be taking on most of the burden for their circulatory systems. That could cause problems down the road. Dr. Elkins, our plastic surgeon, is completing his own tests to determine if he'll need skin stretchers to adequately cover the wounds. As soon as we have that information, we'll know how quickly we can proceed."

At the hospital, Lucy said a distracted goodbye to Nick, her mind consumed with the fact that the children's surgery could take place so soon. She wasn't sure what she'd expected—more tests, more time, more delays. She'd been so prepared for a worst-case scenario that she hadn't planned on returning to work for nearly six months. But she'd just learned that, if all went well, the children could be on their way to recovery before summer.

You can't put it off forever. The children will be adopted. You promised the nuns you'd take care of the arrangements. And when they have their new family, they won't need you anymore.

But today…

Today, they *were* still hers. And they needed her as much as she needed them.

AS SOON AS SHE got back to Nick's, Lucy went straight to the makeshift nursery.

Her heart ached when the children reacted as if they were actually glad to see her, smiling and kicking their little feet.

Taking them from Kyro's arms, she sat down in the rocker and held them close.

Did they have any idea what was happening around them? Could they sense the tension in the air when the doctors and nurses studied them? Did they feel the myriad curious eyes, hear the whispers in the hallways? Were they relieved when they were brought home to their own room and the three women who loved them so much?

Lucy closed her eyes to hold back the tears that gathered and tightened her embrace.

Could they comprehend her desperation as she looked ahead to the dreaded moment when she would have to say goodbye?

Lucy felt the twins moving against her. Faith, the more active of the two, pushed her head away so she could look around, while Hope burrowed beneath Lucy's chin. Though their bodies were joined, their personalities were becoming more and more distinct.

Once the separation was a success—because Lucy couldn't allow herself to think any other way—there would be so many milestones to celebrate. Each girl would grow into herself, discovering all of life's wonders in her own unique way. How wonderful it would be to see the twins crawl for the first time. Walk. Run.

Lucy rubbed her cheek in Hope's hair. Perhaps the adoptive parents would send her pictures.

But even if they did, it wouldn't be the same as…

As adopting them yourself?

Her heart twisted at her own foolishness. As much as she longed to remain close to Faith and Hope, to play an active, intimate part in their lives, considering herself a candidate for their mother didn't make any sense. First of all, the children deserved *two* parents. Even though she hadn't had the girls for long, she'd already seen how challenging raising twins could be. It was rewarding, yes, but there were times when the responsibilities were overwhelming. Added to the obvious stress of caring for two children at once would be the special medical attention required, the need for a stay-at-home mom, stability, consistency.

Even more important, they needed a mother who had a natural talent for nurturing. Lucy had never been the motherly type. She couldn't even nurture a houseplant properly, let alone two living, breathing human beings.

Glancing down, Lucy saw that both children had drifted off to sleep. Moving carefully, she stood and laid them in their crib, then covered them with a soft blanket.

"Sweet dreams, little ones," she whispered.

Lucy stepped into the hall just as Kyro rounded the corner with a basket of fresh laundry heaped with baby things.

"Where is Tamika?"

"She be in her room takin' a nap."

Since Tamika had been awake all of last night with the twins, Lucy was glad the woman had a chance to catch up on her rest.

"The children are asleep, as well."

"All the testing wears them out, poor things." Kyro's eyes searched Lucy's face. "Maybe you should be takin' your own little nap."

Lucy shook her head. "I've got an errand I need to run if you'll be all right."

Kyro balanced the basket on her hip so she could open the nursery door, then made a shooing gesture. "Get on with you. I don't know why you be hirin' the two of us if you won' let us do our jobs."

Lucy smiled ruefully. Having the help of the Tabumba sisters had been the nuns' idea, but Lucy hadn't regretted hiring them for a minute.

Kyro hummed quietly to herself as she entered the nursery. After glancing into the crib, she sat down in the rocker and began to fold the tiny articles of clothing.

There was something Lucy needed to do, and she knew she couldn't put it off much longer. She went into her bedroom, took her phone from her purse, then punched in the number she knew by heart. As she waited, the tension in her stomach increased with every second.

"Jaeger Convalescent Home."

"This is Lucy Devon. I wondered if it would be convenient to visit my mother in the next hour?"

"Yes, of course. She's just finished her lunch, so I'm sure she'd be happy to see you. I'll leave a visitor's pass for you at the reception desk."

"Thank you."

Snapping her phone shut, Lucy rubbed the spot between her eyebrows, hoping to ease the headache that was beginning to build. The time had come to face her mother.

BY THE TIME she pulled in to the circular, tree-lined driveway, Lucy was sick with nerves.

She hadn't seen Lillian Devon since her mother

had been transferred to this facility. Two years ago, after Lucy's father had died of a massive coronary, her mother had collapsed, physically and mentally. The doctor had recommended that Lillian be sent here for long-term care.

Lucy took a deep breath and opened the van door. It pained her that it had proven necessary to move Lillian out of her own home, but her mother's breakdown hadn't been a complete surprise. Although Lillian Devon had remained loyal to her husband until the end, she'd begun withering away soon after Lucy left home.

Clutching a bouquet of flowers, Lucy approached the front desk where she collected her visitor's pass. A nurse volunteered to show her to Lillian's room. Lucy recognized the woman's voice from the many times they'd spoken over the phone.

"How is she?" Lucy asked.

The nurse's shoes squeaked slightly as she and Lucy made their way through the carpeted lounge area. Great care had been taken to give the room a cozy feel, complete with overstuffed furniture, side tables and crocheted doilies.

The nurse sighed. "Physically, she's doing much better. She's not losing weight but she's still too thin. Maybe your visit will cheer her up and help improve her appetite."

Lucy doubted it, but didn't comment.

"As for her mental status," the nurse continued softly, "I'm afraid there hasn't been much change, even with the new medication."

Lucy's heart fell at that news. "Does my mother like it here?"

"She seems…content."

"Meaning that she's still showing very little reaction to anything."

The woman smiled wryly. "Somehow, I think that if she was unhappy, she'd let us know."

"There are times even an angry reaction would be welcome," Lucy said sadly.

The nurse stopped in front of a partially closed door. "Here we are. Just ring the call button if there's anything you need during your visit. Her doctor will be making his rounds shortly, so I'll tell him you're here."

"Thank you."

Lucy waited until the squeaking of the woman's shoes disappeared around the corner before gently tapping on the door and pushing it open.

"Mom?"

A woman sat in a chair next to the window, her body so painfully thin, her hair so white that Lucy couldn't comprehend for a moment that she was looking at her own mother. But as she stepped inside and the door closed behind her, it became clear to Lucy that this visit would be no different from dozens she'd made to the hospital soon after her mother's collapse. Lillian Devon stared blankly out the window, just as she'd done every day since her husband had died.

"Mom, it's Lucy." Lucy placed the flowers in her mother's lap, but Lillian didn't appear to see them or anything else.

Sighing, Lucy knew that trying to engage her mother in a conversation was likely to be as futile as the countless attempts she'd made at talking to her over the phone in the past few months.

Her sorrow quickly gave way to an old familiar anger at her father. This was what happened when a woman allowed herself to care so deeply about a man that she surrendered her very identity to him. Lillian had dedicated her life to her husband. She had given up her own dreams of becoming a writer, her interests and passions—for what? To try to please a man who couldn't be pleased? In return, George Devon had sucked her dry and left her an empty shell.

"Mom, I'll be here in Utah for the next little while. We can see each other every day, if you want."

There was no response. And even though she knew Lillian was locked inside her own depression,

Lucy couldn't help feeling hurt. Once again, her mother was shutting her out.

Taking her mother's hand, Lucy squeezed it.

"Don't worry, Mom. They'll find a way to help you feel better."

But while she said the words, Lucy also understood that her mother's condition was more challenging than that of the twins in many ways. Modern surgery could separate the two little girls, but there was little that doctors could do to mend her mother's bruised and battered soul.

WHEN LUCY RETURNED from the convalescent home, she spent the rest of the afternoon composing a series of lectures she'd volunteered to give at a local university as soon as she'd known she would be spending time in Salt Lake. She'd been forced to turn down such offers so many times in the past that she'd felt obligated to give something back to her alma mater.

By reviewing her career as a journalist and the craft involved in doing her work, Lucy was able to calm herself. She knew she couldn't deny the drive to succeed in her profession—one that was still dominated by men. How could she even think of being anything else at this point?

This was her career.

This was her life, her identity, her calling.

Hadn't her own mother shown her what happened if a person's dreams were deferred or denied?

Her time with Nick and the children was just a short intermission in the life she had chosen. She couldn't allow herself to be lulled into thinking about the might-have-beens. Five years ago, she'd made the right decision in not marrying Nick; nothing had changed. And if Lucy doubted her choice, she had only to look at Lillian to see the pain of a dysfunctional marriage.

After finishing her notes, she'd spent time with the twins, then had retired early. She'd hoped to catch up on some sleep since Tamika would be taking the nighttime feedings. But, so far, her efforts to rest had been unsuccessful. Glancing at the clock on her bedside table, Lucy groaned. Two o'clock.

Since she'd already spent more than an hour tossing and turning, she knew it was useless to lie in bed any longer, her mind whirling in aimless circles, so she swept the covers aside and padded into the bathroom. She changed into her swimsuit, cap and goggles, and grabbed a towel. Then, moving quietly so that she wouldn't disturb the rest of the house, she headed outside.

The night air was cool against her bare shoulders. Even though the temperature had reached the high eighties during the day, it was still early enough in the year for the night to be chilly.

Lucy set her towel on one of the loungers, then dipped a toe in the water. Thankfully, the water was heated, slipping over her skin like silk.

After positioning her goggles, she began swimming laps, hoping that the sheer repetition and physical exertion would help her clear her mind. But after a few minutes she started thinking about Nick Hammond again.

Did he ever come down here when he couldn't sleep? Or did he have other ways to spend a restless night?

From what Lucy had observed since she'd been living with him, she'd assumed that he was committed to life as a single man. But as Lucy spent more time at Primary Children's the hospital staff was opening up to her. According to the medical grapevine, Nick's name had been linked with several women. There were even rumors that he'd proposed to a doctor named Maryann Goss.

But if there was truth to any of the gossip, then why was Nick spending so much time with her? She certainly hadn't seen any evidence of another woman in his life.

It's none of your business. He could be dating the entire female staff of Primary Children's and it still wouldn't be any of your business.

But she couldn't help wondering.

Stop it!

Diving beneath the water, Lucy flipped over, pushing her feet against the wall of the pool and striking out in the opposite direction.

The man is nothing to you. He's a friend and a surgeon, nothing more.

So why was she swimming laps at a punishing pace, knowing that only by reaching the point of utter exhaustion would she be able to put aside her obsession with Nick Hammond long enough to sleep?

NICK STOOD at his bedroom window, watching Lucy as she paused. Clinging to the side of the pool, she gulped for air, her chest rising and falling with the effort to fill her starved lungs. Then, slowly she relaxed and closed her eyes, leaning her head back in the water so that her face was held up to the brightness of the moon.

She was so beautiful.

Beautiful and proud.

And alone.

Bracing a hand on the window frame, Nick found that he couldn't move as she kicked back and floated in the water.

Her swimsuit was strictly utilitarian and not meant to titillate. But the black maillot just emphasized her lithe body and high breasts. Nick was pleased to see that her few weeks in Utah had helped erase the gauntness, and she now appeared lean and healthy.

Very healthy.

Enticing.

Once at the shallow end of the pool, Lucy stood up, adjusting the fit of her goggles. Moonlight and the submerged lamps in the pool cast her body in a silver glow.

So beautiful.

Sinking into the water again, she began swimming, slowly at first. Then, bit by bit, she increased the rhythm of her strokes to the same desperate speed she'd displayed before. Lap after lap, she navigated the pool, moving with the purposefulness of a person who was being pursued.

Was it merely the exercise she craved? Or was it the emotional escape? If so, what demons was she trying to outrun?

Any other time, Nick might have put on his swim trunks and joined her—if only to offer her some company. But something about the way she doggedly continued, then finally stopped at one end and laid her head on her crossed arms and gasped for breath, conveyed to Nick that he would not be welcome.

What was wrong with him? Why couldn't he resolve his feelings for this woman? When Nick had arranged for Lucy to live here for the duration of her stay, his primary motive had been to rid himself of his fascination for her once and for all. He'd been so sure that familiarity would breed contempt.

But with each day that passed, he was forced to admit that his attraction to Lucy was growing, not diminishing.

He was suddenly filled with self-disgust. He knew Lucy would never tie herself to anyone. She was a loner who flourished under the challenges of her work. While he…

He was a man who was tired of being alone.

It wasn't the first time the thought had entered his head, but this time, it had the power to stick.

These weeks with Lucy and the children had taught him that there were trade-offs to a lack of complete freedom. The house was suddenly filled with laughter and vitality. He looked forward to coming home to baby paraphernalia cluttering the counters and the smells of Tamika's freshly baked bread or Lucy's exotic cooking. He didn't even mind that there rarely seemed to be enough hot water or that he was forced to share the remote control on those rare occasions they shared the family room.

He had to keep reminding himself that the situation was temporary. The twins would eventually be adopted, their nurses would return to Africa and Lucy would leave on an assignment to yet another dangerous situation.

So why did he feel so overwhelmed by sadness?

And why couldn't he picture himself sharing this house with anyone other than Lucy?

LUCY'S LUNGS were on fire, her limbs trembling, when she stopped in the deep end and gripped the side of the pool.

Enough. She'd been swimming nonstop for nearly an hour and she was no closer to quieting her incessant worrying. If she was doomed to a sleepless night, she might as well make it productive. With two little ones, there was always something to tidy or organize, bottles to wash. Or she could try her hand at making bread. Tamika had been giving her lessons.

Turning, she swam back to the steps, more slowly this time, her body protesting from its rigorous workout. But as she stood, lifting her hands to wipe the water from her face, she froze, realizing she wasn't alone.

"You should take a break, don't you think?"

She shivered as the cool air swept over her skin. But the gentle rebuke in Nick's tone had far more to do with the gooseflesh that appeared all over her body than the breeze did.

He stood above the steps, wearing little more than a pair of low-slung pajama bottoms. The underwater pool lights danced over his tight abdomen and broad chest.

"I told myself I wouldn't come down here. But as you can see, I lost my own argument."

The shaking in Lucy's limbs increased, so much so that she feared she wouldn't be able to get out of the water without help.

"Come here, Lucy," he said tenderly, holding out a hand.

She forced herself to move, feeling the tug of gravity as she stepped from the water, and willingly accepted the support Nick offered. And when, after only a split second's hesitation, he pulled her into his embrace, she could not resist. She clung to his shoulders, resting her head against his chest.

"Dear God, how I've missed you, Lucy."

The words were spoken so softly that Lucy wasn't sure she'd heard them correctly. Surely, Nick Hammond would never admit such a thing.

When he slipped his arms beneath her legs and carried her into the house, she still didn't resist. It wasn't until he started up the stairs that she lifted her head and made a sound of protest.

"To sleep. Only to sleep."

Once in the bedroom, he set her on the ground and pointed her in the direction of his bathroom. "Dry off in there. You'll find T-shirts in the bottom drawer and my robe on the back of the door."

Lucy supposed she should do something, say something. Object. But at the moment, she couldn't think. She could only feel—feel the lingering warmth of his body against her skin, the delicious languor that had settled in her limbs.

She did as he suggested, donning a soft well-washed shirt and the voluminous robe. Then, unaccountably self-conscious, she opened the door.

Nick was waiting. He reached out and drew her to the bed. She climbed between the sheets and blankets, dropping her head on the fluffy pillows.

"I should—"

"Shh," he interrupted. "Sleep. We're just going to sleep."

"But Tamika and Kyro—"

"I don't think they'll fit. They'll have to stay in their own beds."

Against her will, she smiled. Deep down, she knew this night would lead to complications and that, for pride's sake, she should feign a few more objections. But as Nick settled against her and they spooned together in the darkness, she found she couldn't speak.

She could only surrender to a pleasant drowsiness and the feeling that all was suddenly right with the world.

Chapter Eight

To Lucy's infinite relief, she woke to find that Nick had left for work, and Tamika, Kyro and the twins were still fast asleep.

Skulking into her bedroom like a thief afraid of being caught, she quickly showered and dressed. Then, since she could hear stirring in the other room, she decided that she wouldn't try to return the clothes she'd borrowed. Instead, she hung them in the back of the closet behind her own things.

After checking on the girls, she wandered over to the corner of the kitchen that she'd staked out as her work space.

Knowing she couldn't put off the task any longer, Lucy began to riffle through the papers the hospital social worker had provided on the numerous adoption agencies in the area.

She knew she should already have found a family for the girls. At the very least, she should've chosen an agency.

But as she stared at the list, she couldn't bring herself to pick up the phone. Calling one of the adoption facilitators would make things so…formal. So final.

Lucy sighed. It didn't matter that time was working against her and that preparations needed to be made. Her life had begun to revolve around the girls so much that she couldn't imagine their being gone.

Lucy shoved the papers back into their file folders. Not today. She would wait a little longer—at least until she knew when the surgery would be performed. An agency would probably need that information, anyway.

But as she escaped to the nursery, she couldn't ignore the dread she felt waiting for the moment when she could no longer delay the inevitable.

IN THE DAYS that followed, Lucy concentrated on settling into a routine. In the morning, she helped with the girls' feeding. Then she made her way to the university to give two lectures and once she was finished there, she stopped by the convalescent home to see her mother. Lillian was beginning to respond to the new medication and Lucy's regular visits. She'd begun to take walks in the garden and socialize with the other residents. And when Lucy arrived, she was eager for a long chat and a report of Lucy's day. By late afternoon, Lucy returned for hospital appointments, naptime and to play with the girls.

And yet...the twins weren't the only focus of her attention. She found herself wondering when Nick would arrive home, what they would talk about during dinner and whether or not he would join her for laps in the pool as had become their ritual since the night they'd slept in his bed.

Lucy knew she was treading on dangerous ground. She had sworn to herself that she wouldn't rely on him in anything but a professional capacity. She'd told herself again and again that the relationship they'd shared was over and she didn't have the right—or the energy—to feel anything else for Nick.

But he only had to step into the room for her pulse to quicken. And when he joined her at the pool, his body sculpted like an athlete's, she grew hot all over.

Didn't she have any pride? Couldn't she see that she was falling into the same familiar trap? Yes, Nick's nearness had the power to make her feel alive in a way that she couldn't deny. But such joy could also bring great pain. Passion was intense but fleeting.

Besides, Nick clearly didn't feel anything for her

other than a warm fondness. The fact that he never tempted her to return to his bed—not even just to sleep—was proof enough of that.

As the girls' tests increased in frequency and detail, he retreated behind a mask of professionalism. There were times Lucy could've sworn she caught a flash of awareness deep in his eyes, leading her to believe that he wasn't as unaffected as he might seem. But he made no overtures to touch her.

Sighing, Lucy knew she should be relieved. But to her shame, she longed for the heat of his caress and a release of the desire that simmered inside her.

That her emotions were so out of control was infinitely disturbing. She was terrified of what might happen if she surrendered to her longings and kept reminding herself that her energy should be centered on the children, that if Nick touched her, her hunger might become all-consuming.

But her arguments were growing thin. With each day away from her job, she was confronted by everything she'd missed in the past few years. She had spent so much time in war-ravaged regions of the world that she'd forgotten how beautiful life could be.

"Lucy?"

Her head shot up at Nick's voice.

Why hadn't she heard him come in?

She automatically smoothed her hair, and Lucy cursed herself. It didn't matter what she looked like. She wasn't trying to impress him.

Nevertheless, when he appeared at the entrance to the nursery her heart skipped a beat.

Nick leaned his shoulder against the doorjamb and studied her for several long seconds without speaking.

"D-did you need something?"

He shook his head. "You're looking better. You must be eating well."

Couldn't he think of anything else to talk about? But Lucy guessed her weight was a safe topic compared to many of the other things they could discuss.

Seeking an equally innocuous subject to continue the conversation, she settled on, "Are you finished for the day?"

He nodded, folding his arms across his chest. "Amazingly enough, I am."

She waited, still wondering why he'd sought her out, but he seemed content just to stand there, taking in the sunny confines of the nursery, the babies sleeping in the crib and Lucy sitting with her legs drawn up beneath her in the overstuffed rocking chair.

"Was there something you wanted?" she prompted, an effervescent tension filling her veins.

"I've been thinking…." He straightened, then sauntered into the room with the grace of an animal on the prowl. "You and the girls have been spending a lot of time cooped up here or at the hospital. The weather is warmer now, and… How would you like to go on an outing?"

Her heart leaped at the mere thought of spending time with Nick. She'd done her best to avoid him, yet now, when she had the opportunity to refuse, she couldn't say no.

"I'd like that." The words slipped out, almost of their own volition.

"The girls are probably too young for the zoo, so I thought we could take them on a picnic, then go for a walk with their stroller."

"That would be perfect."

"What about Tamika and Kyro? Do you think they'd like to come?"

As much as she thought she should avoid being alone with Nick, Lucy knew she had to be honest. "I'm sure they would, but if we're taking the girls, they'd probably like to go back to the hospital," she said hesitantly. "They've been excited about their volunteer work there."

He nodded. "Fine. Then I'll get a picnic ready for two."

After he left the room, it took several minutes for her pulse to return to normal. When it did, she inhaled a deep, calming breath.

She was insane to willingly spend time alone with this man.

But she couldn't find the will to refuse.

NICK KNEW he was a fool. Since the night he'd slept with Lucy in his arms, he'd done his best to remain on a professional footing with her. Over and over again, he'd sworn to himself that he'd put his feelings for her behind him. They would be friends—nothing more. But with each day that passed, it was becoming increasingly difficult.

What was wrong with him? Heaven only knew that any sort of lasting relationship with Lucy Devon was out of the question.

As he entered the kitchen and opened the refrigerator, Nick frowned. He was either crazy or a glutton for punishment. After all, it had been his idea to insist that Lucy and the twins stay here. But he'd been so sure that prolonged contact would help lessen his attraction to her.

Unfortunately, the opposite had been true. He craved time with Lucy—so much so, that he now knew his feelings for her were not going to be easily defeated. Worse yet, he was beginning to discover that it wasn't just the thought of a physical relationship that tempted him.

He wanted more. He wanted to come home to her

each evening, spend time reading in the same room, talking about music and doing the Sunday cross-word together. He liked having dinner waiting for him every once in a while, or a note explaining the whereabouts of the "women in his life."

Yet, in getting a sense of what it would be like to have Lucy as his wife and the mother of his children, Nick was repeatedly confronted with Lucy's emotional defenses. If they were to consider renewing their relationship…

No.

Nick shut the refrigerator door with a determined thump. He shouldn't even think about it.

Marriage? He really had gone off the deep end. He didn't want to marry Lucy. He was happy with his life the way it was. He might be tempted to in-dulge in a…romantic involvement while Lucy was here, but that didn't mean he wanted to make it per-manent. He had to keep his mind focused on the twins and their condition.

But even as he reminded himself of that, Nick had to admit he'd already passed the point where things could be that simple. In the space of a few weeks, he'd grown immensely protective and possessive of Lucy and the children.

"Any luck?"

Nick's thoughts dispersed like blowing sand as

Lucy approached him from behind. Even from a few feet away, he was sure he could detect the warmth of her body and the scent of her perfume. French perfume. The expensive stuff. Yet, dressed in capri pants and a T-shirt, she wore the fragrance as casually as a dime-store cologne, making the incongruity that much more tantalizing.

"What would you like to eat?"

She shrugged. "I'm starving, so I'm not too particular."

He walked to the phone book. "Exotic or all-American?" he asked.

"Surprise me."

He ran a finger down the listings, ignoring the temptation to suggest, "a jug of wine and thou."

But a quick glance at Lucy confirmed that such a suggestion wouldn't be welcome. She was clearly having second thoughts about accompanying him for the afternoon, let alone doing anything more…romantic.

"Get the kids together, okay? I'll take a shower and meet you in twenty minutes."

LUCY WAS WAITING for Nick in the living room when he appeared at the bottom of the stairs wearing jeans, sneakers and a polo shirt.

Lucy felt a shiver course down her spine. When

he wore his shirt and tie to the hospital he was devastatingly handsome, but like this—tousled and relaxed—he was irresistible.

"What are you watching?" he asked, gesturing to the television.

Lucy flushed. She'd tuned in to CNC out of habit. For the past week, she'd been keeping tabs on Erik Parker and the hostage drama unfolding in Colombia.

"Nothing, really." She hurriedly reached for the remote, but before she had a chance to turn off the TV, he took the device from her hand and stared at the screen.

"What a mess," he murmured after listening to Erik Parker explain that another fifteen people had been taken hostage, including nine Americans. Nick pointed to the correspondent. "Do you know that guy?"

"Yes." The word shot out like a bullet, causing Nick to look at her questioningly. "He's new" was the only explanation she offered.

"And you don't like him."

She shrugged with as much casualness as she could muster. "I've never worked with Erik Parker."

"But you don't like him," Nick said.

She shoved her hands in her pockets. "He's new, he's brash, he's hungry, and he's after my job. Other than that, he's fine."

Nick's eyes twinkled in amusement, then narrowed suddenly. Pointing to the screen, he said, "This is the assignment they wanted you to take a few weeks ago, isn't it?"

"Yes."

"And you didn't accept."

She rolled her eyes. "I'm here, aren't I?"

"But you wanted to go."

She opened her mouth to refuse, but hesitated. She didn't know what she'd wanted then—or what she wanted now, for that matter. Her career was such an integral part of her life, it was difficult letting go, even temporarily.

Especially to someone like Erik Parker.

"My place is here."

She'd hoped her response would curtail any more questions, but Nick wasn't satisfied.

"It's killing you, isn't it—being out of the thick of things?"

"No," she said proudly. "I'm perfectly happy being here and helping the twins."

"I'm sure you are. But aren't you a little jealous of Parker?"

"I think Parker is a pretty boy in a Brooks Brothers suit, but I'm not about to trot off to Colombia to relieve him of his duties."

"What if someone called today, told you that you

were needed, that Parker had…dysentery or some-thing, and you were the only person who could take his place. You wouldn't be tempted to hop a flight to Colombia?"

"Not in the least."

"I see. Then you won't be needing this." He re-moved a piece of yellow paper from his jeans pocket and held it in the air with two fingers.

"What is it?"

"It's a phone message from Frank Carlisle. Erik Parker has contracted amoebic dysentery. He's barely been able to stand long enough to do his re-ports. They need a replacement ASAP and they want you to fly to Colombia."

Her fingers curled into her palms as she fought for control. She was at once piqued at Nick for bait-ing her and at herself for being curious about the phone call she'd missed.

"Wait a minute," she said slowly. "How on earth did you end up taking a phone message from Frank Carlisle?"

"He said to tell you that your cell phone's broken and to get it fixed. I guess when he couldn't reach you, he contacted the only other person whose name he knew. Me."

She growled in frustration, snatching the mes-sage away from Nick and crumpling it into a ball.

"Frank Carlisle needs to learn to take no for an answer," Lucy said in a dire tone. Then she marched into the foyer and threw the scrap of paper into the brass wastebasket. Bending to pick up the children's carrier she said, "Let's go. I'm starved."

Whistling softly, Nick followed her out the door, his gaze lingering on the phone message she'd tossed into the trash.

He wasn't sure what he'd expected when he'd informed Lucy about the call, but having her toss the note into the garbage certainly wasn't it.

In a way, Nick had been testing her. Over the past few evenings, he'd noticed that Lucy had been paying more and more attention to CNC, particularly when the situation in Colombia was being reported. It hadn't taken him long to connect the dots—and Nick surmised that Lucy was torn between her need to be with the twins and her desire to get back to a job she loved.

What saddened him was that he knew it was only a matter of time before she returned to the field. He'd merely had to be sure that she wasn't contemplating an exit anytime soon.

Nick stopped next to the van where Lucy was buckling in the carrier.

"Will you put the stroller in back?" she asked.

"Certainly."

From inside the van, Lucy watched as he folded up the stroller and slid it into the cargo area. She was about to step down when he moved in front of her.

"Keys?"

Since she was already irritated with Nick and the way he'd baited her inside the house, his assumption that he would be driving rankled. Because he was a man, he simply assumed that he should take charge. Why? Why did he always have to be the one in control? He was like her father had been, always taking control, never thinking about what she might like, how she might feel.

Lucy knew that her reaction bordered on childish, but she tightened her fingers around the keys.

"I can manage."

"We need to pick up our lunch and it might be easier if—"

"I can manage."

At her implacable tone, he held up his hands in surrender. "Fine."

For a long moment, he didn't move, making her achingly aware of his lean, powerful body. If he were to reach for her, pull her into his arms…

She wouldn't be able to resist.

Despite her best efforts to retain her equilibrium, Lucy felt herself gravitating toward him ever so slightly. As if acknowledging her unspoken invitation, his hands spanned her waist and lifted her to the ground. Then, when he could have stepped away, he didn't.

"You're good with the children."

An utterly innocent remark, but spoken so softly, right next to her ear, that it could have been a caress.

"They're young, and not too much trouble. They still spend a lot of time sleeping."

"And you dote on them even when they're asleep."

She felt a flush steal up her cheeks, even though she knew there was nothing really embarrassing about his remark. Nevertheless, it bothered her that he might think she was weak in any way. She'd spent a lifetime building a front of steel to protect her in both her career and her relationships and felt uncomfortable letting him see her less than fully guarded.

"The girls obviously respond well to you. They've gained several pounds since they arrived."

She couldn't help beaming. "Yes, it's wonderful! Dr. Granger says they're thinking of removing the tubes in a few days."

"I know."

She bit her lip, realizing that of course Nick knew. He was even better informed than she was about the twins' condition.

Silence fell between them, but he remained close—so close that she could smell his woodsy combination of soap and cologne and see every furrow his comb had made in his wet hair.

Inexplicably, her fingers twitched with the desire to reach up and touch the severely tamed strands, to finger-comb them into a more casual style.

"You've changed, Lucy," Nick said, his voice so low that she nearly missed the words.

"No. I'm the same."

He shook his head. "You seem…more comfortable in your own skin."

And how was she supposed to take that?

"I—I don't know what you mean."

He lifted one of his hands and traced his finger down the curve of her cheek.

"You've lost the chip on your shoulder."

She huffed in indignation. "I never had a chip on my shoulder!"

"Oh, but you did. You were always so intent on proving to everyone that you were entirely self-sufficient."

"I'd hardly call that a chip."

"It is if it's taken to the extreme."

She frowned. "I didn't ask for help because I didn't need it."

"Perhaps I wanted to give it," he said, his thumb

stroking her lips. His words cut her to the core. "Everyone needs to be needed, Lucy. There's no shame in allowing another person to care for you."

Outwardly, Lucy remained still, but she cringed on the inside. Was that really what he'd thought? That she had never *needed* him?

"If you felt that way," she asked, "why didn't you say something?"

His eyes had grown shadowed. "Because it was obvious that it would only make everything worse."

She looked down, focusing on a button on his polo shirt, her jaw stiffening. "So it's completely my fault that things didn't work out between us?"

"No, I'm not saying that. We both had…unresolvable issues that we failed to communicate."

She opened her mouth to insist that she hadn't left anything unsaid, but closed it again. It would be the height of denial if she protested. She'd met him at the courthouse to tell him she was leaving him. The only explanation she'd offered was her job. But there'd been other things she hadn't wanted to admit to herself….

"I think it's time we were going," she said firmly, moving away from him and sliding into the front seat.

Not until it was too late did she realize she'd claimed the passenger side rather than the driver's as she'd originally planned.

Chapter Nine

Despite Lucy's rattled nerves, the day proved to be perfect for a picnic. Warm sun streamed down from a cloudless, azure sky. A gentle breeze prevented it from getting too hot and the air was redolent with the scent of flowers and newly mowed grass.

Nick chose a small, picturesque park nestled in Immigration Canyon. Situated in a tranquil pine grove, next to a bubbling creek, the spot gave the illusion of being hidden deep in the mountains.

As Nick unloaded the stroller and the twins, Lucy laid a cloth over a wooden table and began spreading out the food Nick had chosen. To her delight, there was a crusty loaf of bread, rounds of focaccia, exotic sliced cheeses and deli meats, huge kosher pickles, marinated olives, fresh fruit and iced sodas.

"Still on call?" she asked, referring to the pager clipped to his belt.

"I'm always on call," Nick grumbled. But there was no heat to his complaint. It was obvious that he didn't mind the arrangement.

He placed the stroller in the shade and grinned as the children stared up at the majestic green pine trees and the blue sky overhead.

"They like it," he commented as they blinked in wonder.

"They're growing so fast. Lately, they're spending more and more time awake."

"Good. That means they'll be ready for their surgery on the fifteenth."

It took several long seconds for the words to sink in. When they did, Lucy looked up at him, a package of plastic utensils dropping nervously from her fingers.

"What?" she breathed, sure that if she spoke too loudly, she would discover she'd imagined his words.

"The twins' surgery has been scheduled for the fifteenth. All the data we've been collecting has been plugged into a virtual simulator that a local development company has been testing. As a team, we'll practice the operation again and again until we've perfected our approach. By the fifteenth we should be ready for the real thing."

Lucy rushed toward him, throwing her arms

around his neck. "Is this really, truly going to happen? And so quickly?"

He nodded, stroking her hair. "We're concerned about Faith's heart. To delay much longer could cause further problems for her. Dr. Elkins is convinced that he can perform the plastic-surgery end of the procedure without the need for skin stretchers, so we're going ahead."

Tears sprang to Lucy's eyes and she clung to Nick for support. So much of her energy had been devoted toward attaining this goal. Now that they'd reached it, her limbs trembled and threatened to give way.

"We're not out of the woods yet, Lucy. For the next couple of weeks, you'll probably spend more time in and out of the hospital than you already have. When we begin to use the simulator, we'll have more refined data, and we'll be monitoring the girls every day. And I don't need to warn you about the seriousness of the procedure itself."

"I know, I know. I'm just so…grateful."

He tightened his arms around her, and she felt a kiss brush her ear.

"They're fighters, Lucy. If anyone has a chance, they do."

"Thank you," she whispered. Compelled by her emotions, she rose on tiptoe and pressed a kiss to his lips.

It was hesitant at first, as they both measured the repercussions. But then, unable to turn away from temptation, Lucy kissed him again…and again.

When they were both breathing heavily, Nick lifted his head.

"We'd better eat," he said, his voice tight with passion.

"Yes," she agreed, suddenly remembering that they were in a public park. "Let's eat."

But neither of them moved. Instead, Lucy rested her head on Nick's chest and he responded by kissing her gently.

For a moment, she felt safe.

She felt loved.

She squeezed her eyes closed in an attempt to deny the emotion that swelled within her. Lucy knew full well she was playing with fire. She couldn't become involved with this man again. Nothing had changed. In a few months she would return to her job and her life as a single woman.

But even as she inwardly chided herself for her foolishness, it was clear there was no point.

She was already on the brink of falling in love again.

IT WAS NEARLY MIDNIGHT before silence offered Lucy the opportunity she'd been waiting for.

Everyone was asleep.

Carefully opening her bedroom door, she crept through the hall to the foyer, then bent in front of the wastepaper basket and retrieved the phone message written by Nick's receptionist.

Parker is sick with amoebic dysentery. I need someone with experience in Colombia—now! *Call me. I'll throw in a bonus if you'll do it.*

As she stared into the blackness, Lucy pondered what to do next. If she called Frank—just to let him know that she'd received the message—he would use every argument he could muster to get her to go to Colombia. And even though she had no intention of leaving the twins, she knew herself well enough to anticipate the guilt he would inspire.

And she knew that part of her would wish she could accept his offer.

A rush of shame washed over her, but she didn't have the will to deny the truth. For so long, her work had been everything to her. Although she loved taking care of the twins, she also missed her job, the rush of adrenaline, the constant demands.

No.

She couldn't think about that now. Faith and Hope were her only concerns. She wouldn't trade a moment in their company for the satisfaction her work gave her, not when each day was so precious.

Standing up, Lucy slid the paper into the pocket of her robe and sneaked back to her room....

Never seeing Nick, who'd been poised at the top of the stairs, watching every move she made.

SCOWLING, NICK RETREATED into his room, deciding against a quick snack. He wasn't hungry anymore.

As he closed his door and sank onto the bed, Nick tried to rid his mind of what he'd witnessed, but try as he might, he couldn't banish the sight of Lucy poring over the message. A message she'd retrieved in the dead of night when she'd thought no one else would be awake.

A familiar resentment settled in his stomach like a lead weight. As much as he kept telling himself that he wasn't involved with Lucy and didn't intend to become involved with her, he knew it was already too late. Once again, he'd begun to...care for Lucy. Seeing her work come between them, just as it had the first time, filled him with frustration and anger. At himself and at her. He needed her to remain focused on the children. She couldn't be flying off to Colombia now.

But as Nick silently railed against Lucy and her career, he knew he was being unfair. He had no evidence that she'd shortchanged the children in any way—or that she would in the future. With surgery approaching, he doubted she'd suddenly desert them.

But that didn't mean she wouldn't leave as soon as the children had begun to recover.

Remember that. She won't be staying. So keep your mind on your job and off Lucy Devon. Stay away from her unless she's with the twins.

Punching his pillow, Nick fell back on the bed and sighed—because even as he made these promises to himself, he knew he would end up breaking them.

As May turned into June, Lucy looked back on that day with Nick as a moment of peace in the midst of a storm of activity.

With preparations for the surgery in full swing, Lucy was growing accustomed to the increased number of hospital visits. She was soon on a first-name basis with the members of the surgical team, the nursing staff, several social workers and most of the administration. Indeed, the broad corridors of Primary Children's Medical Center were beginning to feel like a home away from home in some respects. Lord only knew they'd spent enough time there—and would spend much more in the days to come.

Handling all the appointments had become a full-time job for Lucy, but it wasn't without its rewards.

Each day, she watched the children grow stronger and the possibility of a separation inch closer to reality. She loved listening to the twins' hearts beating in unison over the sound monitors—Faith and Hope had come into the world joined together, and now they were fighting for a future apart.

And what about me? Lucy wondered. *I used to know what was worth fighting for in my life. But now...*

She felt as if she was at a crossroads, and she didn't know where to turn next. Her need for Nick was growing beyond what she could bear. And her love for the children bordered on the possessiveness of a lioness for her cubs. She would do anything for her girls. *Anything.*

But she was so afraid of making a mistake. She knew firsthand how devastating it could be to get mixed up in someone else's problems. She couldn't—*wouldn't*—allow that to happen to Nick or the children.

And so, just as she'd always ended up at her mother's side when she needed help, Lucy decided to make the trip across town to the Jaeger Convalescent Home. Even with all her troubles, Lillian had loved Lucy as best she could, and for that Lucy was grateful. She felt as though she needed that unconditional love now.

"Mom?"

Lucy opened the door to her mother's room and peered inside.

Lillian Devon sat at a table, and Lucy immediately noticed that she seemed "clearer" today, just as the nurse had said. The new medication had helped to lift Lillian out of her paralyzing depression. She'd begun to take regular walks through the gardens and join other residents for meals in the dining room. But Lucy sensed that her own visits had helped as well. It touched her heart that her mother's eyes brightened when she saw her.

Today another milestone had been reached. Rather than staring despondently out the window, Lillian had dressed in a pair of jeans and a sweater and was sitting by the window playing solitaire with a deck of worn cards.

Lucy couldn't count the number of times she'd seen her mother play the game. Something about that activity had always had the power to center Lillian, but at the same time, her concentration caused her to appear distant and unapproachable, especially to a young child.

"Mom, I've brought someone with me to visit."

Pushing the door back, Lucy wheeled the stroller into the room.

At first, her mother didn't look up from her game.

But when she finally did, her eyes locked on to the baby carriage, and her mouth parted in surprise.

Knowing she'd momentarily captured her mother's interest, Lucy pushed the stroller closer.

"I would like to introduce Faith and Hope."

Slowly, ever so slowly, her mother set the cards on the table and leaned forward to get a better look at the babies.

Lucy bit her lip, not really knowing how her mother would react to seeing the girls. In the months she'd been with them, Lucy had witnessed many different reactions—from pity to shock to fear.

But Lillian smiled, warming Lucy from within. When was the last time Lillian had smiled in her presence?

"May I hold them?"

Her mother's voice held the timidity of a child.

"Yes, of course."

Lucy lifted the twins and settled them in her mother's arms.

Lillian's hands shook as she stroked their fluffy hair and patted first one back, then the other.

"Beautiful," she sighed. Then, standing, she moved to a flowered rocker and began to rock the children.

A tightness gripped Lucy's throat at the tenderness of the scene. But not wanting to lose the opportunity to encourage her mother to interact, she began telling Lillian the whole story of how she'd come to be the children's guardian and how she'd fought to bring them to the United States.

The more she talked, the easier it became to open up. She told Lillian how she'd enlisted Nick's help and described the progress with the children's planned surgery. Yet, when it came time to tell Lillian about the need to find them adoptive parents, she hesitated. Gazing at her mother and the delighted expression she wore as she held the twins, Lucy knew it was far too early to mention anything of that nature.

At Lillian's request, they took the children for a stroll through the garden and then into the common area for lemonade and homemade cookies. The refreshments seemed to be a none-too-subtle excuse for Lillian to introduce the children to the other women.

Later, when Lillian showed signs of tiring, Lucy escorted her mother to her room, then wrapped the twins in a blanket. But when she was about to leave, Lillian caught her wrist.

"Come back again tomorrow, won't you? I've enjoyed our visit."

"Yes, of course. I'll bring the children with me."

Her mother smiled at her. "I would love that. But

you don't always have to bring them along. Our times alone have been special, too."

A warmth spread through Lucy's chest and she squeezed Lillian's hand. "Thanks, Mom. I'll see you tomorrow."

AFTER SPENDING so much time with Nick and the other surgeons, Lucy knew all too well the risks the surgery carried. One or both of the twins could die, and the thought haunted her.

During those dark hours, it was Nick who unwittingly provided her with the most comfort. He was always quick to reassure Lucy that every possible measure had been taken to ensure the twins' well-being.

Through it all, their attraction simmered barely below the surface. On several occasions, it became overwhelming, and Nick pulled her to him for a fiery kiss. It was only while he held her in his arms that she felt truly safe and allowed herself to believe that everything would be all right. Yet Lucy knew she was foolish to let her happiness depend on another person.

After the surgery I'll worry about that, Lucy thought, holding the children close and absently rocking them as she stared out the window, waiting for the sight of Nick's headlights to signal that he was home.

Finally, she saw the beams wash over the driveway.

"He's here," she whispered to the twins.

Lucy wasn't the only person who reacted to Nick's homecoming. The moment they heard his voice, the girls would seek him out and smile.

Tomorrow's the day, Lucy reminded herself as she got up to meet Nick. Twenty-four hours from now, the surgery could very well be over.

And the fates of my two little girls will be set in motion.

Lucy crossed into the kitchen just as Nick opened the door. She marveled at the way—even with everything else on her mind—her pulse leaped at the mere sight of him.

"How did things go today?" she asked, referring to the final practice session the team had had that day.

"Smooth as glass. Let's hope tomorrow does, too." He set his keys and briefcase on the counter, then bent to give each of the girls a kiss.

"Any problems on your end?"

She shook her head. During the afternoon, she'd taken the children to the hospital for their last evaluations. The girls had been banded for their upcoming stay.

"Where are Tamika and Kyro?"

"Some of the nurses from the pediatrics wing invited them to a barbecue. They were so wound up, I thought they might as well try to have some fun and get their minds off their worries."

Nick touched her cheek. "What about your worries?"

"I'd rather spend a quiet evening at home with Faith and Hope."

"May I join you?"

She nodded, her throat tightening. "We would all like that."

"How about if I do the cooking tonight?"

She grinned. "Meaning more takeout?"

"Nah. Let's have our own little barbecue."

"That sounds good." She hesitated, then said, "I've been thinking a lot about what...could go wrong."

Nick opened his mouth to speak, but Lucy held up a hand. "I'm not brooding over things, just accepting that there's risk."

"Go on."

"Well, I began to think that I needed to give the children something—something special—just in case..." She rushed on, unable to state her fears aloud. "Since birth, each of the twins has had to contend with the added weight of being attached to the other. I wondered if it might be possible to...to take them into the pool with us tonight. To give them a few minutes of buoyancy and a little free-dom."

Nick's eyes filled with such gentleness that Lucy nearly lost her grip on her chaotic emotions.

"I think that would be a wonderful idea."

"It won't…hurt anything?"

"I think they'd enjoy it."

Lucy gave him a tremulous smile. "I bought them some swim diapers and Kyro helped me adapt them."

"Why don't all of you go get dressed? I'll get changed myself and meet you by the pool. After we've given the girls a chance to splash around, we'll worry about our food."

BY THE TIME LUCY made it out to the backyard, Nick was already in the pool. As she stepped into the warm water, holding the children, he took her arm in support. Then, after allowing the girls to grow accustomed to the strange situation, they moved where it was deeper so Lucy and Nick could stand and hold the babies between them.

Hope slapped the water with her palm, then blinked in astonishment when it splashed her in the face. Faith, on the other hand, seemed highly suspi-cious of the entire arrangement, her lower lip jutting out and her chin quivering. But within a few minutes, both girls were wriggling and burbling, thoroughly enjoying themselves.

When Nick took the babies and kicked back in the water to swim in a slow circle, Lucy watched with tears streaming uncontrollably down her face. No matter what happened, she knew she would always remember this night. This was what other families took for granted—a few stolen moments spent playing in the water.

Nick began to swim toward her and she quickly wiped her cheeks, hoping he'd attribute any moisture to the activity in the pool.

"We should probably get the girls out now," he said, handing them to her. "I wouldn't want them to get chilled."

"I'll go rinse them in a warm shower and put them in their pajamas."

"While you're doing that, I'll get started on the food."

It took her less than twenty minutes to ensure that all the chlorine had been washed away and to dress the girls in their footed pajamas. But even before the adapted Velcro fasteners could be drawn closed, the twins were asleep—Hope on her back and Faith curling toward her sister, her fingers on Hope's cheek.

After setting them in the crib and pulling a blanket over their chests, Lucy gave each of them a kiss, then tiptoed from the room.

When she rejoined Nick, she had changed into a pair of denim cropped pants and a white T-shirt. She laughed when she discovered he was similarly dressed in a pair of navy shorts and a white polo shirt.

"We look like we're dressed for a family photo." The moment the words escaped, she wished she could retrieve them. She didn't need to be reminded that—although they lived under the same roof—they weren't a family.

"I've got steak and chicken. I thought I'd make some kebabs with roasted vegetables."

"Sounds delicious. What should I do to help?"

"Just sit and relax. I found a salad in the refrigerator that Kyro made last night and some of Tamika's bread. Then there's fruit, cheese and some leftover cake from the weekend. Altogether, we should have something of a feast."

Lucy relaxed on one of the lounge chairs, enjoying the balmy evening. She'd heard a great deal of talk about their "unseasonably warm June weather." But after spending more than one summer in the deserts of the Persian Gulf or the jungles of Africa and the Amazon, she found the temperatures here downright comfortable.

Within an hour, the food was ready and they stood

with laden plates. But instead of sitting down at the picnic table with its brightly colored umbrella, Lucy met Nick's eyes.

"I would almost rather—"

"—eat inside with the twins," he finished. "Let's go."

They carried the food indoors where Lucy spread a blanket on the nursery-room floor for their impromptu picnic. There, by the soft glow of a rabbit-shaped night-light, they ate and quietly talked.

"Do you have any questions about tomorrow?"

"I think I'm clear on all the medical procedures. The questions I have can only be answered by the way events unfold afterward."

Not for the first time, Nick said, "They're fighters. In cases like these, that's half the battle."

"They've already had to endure so many obstacles."

Nick squeezed her hand. "Those obstacles have served to make them even stronger."

"Yes, I suppose."

When they'd finished eating, Nick took their plates to the kitchen and returned. He sat down beside Lucy, pulling her close.

She laid her ear over his heart, drawing strength from its steady beat.

"How long before their next feeding?"

"At least a couple of hours."

"Then we've got a little time alone...."

Chapter Ten

She and Nick spent the next two hours in each other's arms, dozing lightly until the children woke. From then on, they devoted their attention to the girls, enjoying the twins' last burst of energy before they settled down for the night.

The evening was bittersweet as she and Nick cherished what could be the girls' final hours. As time seemed to slip through her fingers, Lucy reflected on everything that had brought her to this point. She marveled at her naiveté when she'd originally believed she could remain objective through all the proceedings. At that moment, her feelings for the children were far from detached. She loved them more than she would ever have thought possible.

When the twins fell asleep in her arms close to midnight, she could no longer contain her emotions. Quickly placing them in the crib, she began to sob—

huge, piteous sobs that came from the depths of her heart. Without warning, she felt Nick's arms around her.

"Shh, shh," he whispered against the top of her head.

"I'm so afraid."

"I know."

She was infinitely grateful that he didn't offer her platitudes, or promises that were beyond his ability to fulfill. Instead, he simply held her tight, rocking her from side to side, instilling her with his own strength.

"I'll do everything in my power to help them. You know that, don't you, Lucy?"

She nodded. In his arms she felt a measure of comfort and safety that she had never experienced before. But as her fears subsided, she found herself overwhelmed by an even more primitive emotion.

She wanted this man, body and soul. The thought was at once humbling and arousing. But admitting her needs was one thing, acting on them was another.

Automatically, she pushed against the arms that encircled her. But as she did so, her soul ached all the more.

"I don't want to leave you," she whispered.

"Then don't."

She squeezed her eyes shut and rested her head on his chest. "Things are already so complicated…."

"They don't have to be."

"I'm so tired—tired of worrying, tired of bearing the burdens alone."

"Then don't take all this on yourself. I'm here for you, Lucy. I've always been here for you."

She looked up then, meeting his eyes. And in that moment, she knew she didn't have the strength to resist the urgings of her own heart. She needed this man. She'd always needed him. She'd just been too blind and too frightened to admit the truth.

Unable to speak, she touched his cheek, his lips, his eyebrows. Then, tilting her face up, she pulled his head toward her as he bent to kiss her.

In an instant, their desire became impossible to deny. Nick's arms swept around her waist, taking her weight as her knees threatened to give way.

"We shouldn't be doing this," she gasped when he drew back to trail a line of kisses down her neck.

"Why not?"

Why not?

She couldn't think of a logical answer. Indeed, she couldn't think of anything at all as he spread his hands across her back, pulling her even more tightly against him.

"I've missed you, Lucy," he sighed.

The words warmed her from the inside out, adding a honeyed sweetness to the desire that raged within her.

"I've missed you, too."

"Not just because of *this*—granted, it's nice…"

She chuckled. "I know what you mean."

He drew back again, his expression grave. "Do you? I'm not sure I even understand myself." He framed her face with his hands. "When you left me on our wedding day, I was so angry, so…hurt…"

Lucy had never known a man who would admit such things to himself, let alone utter them aloud.

"Over the years I've tried to convince myself that I've moved on, but the past few weeks have shown me how miserably I've failed," he continued. "I love coming home to you. I love the way you make me feel when you smile at me. I love hearing you sing in the kitchen and the way you talk to yourself when you're concentrating."

So why hadn't he loved her enough all those years ago to understand why she'd refused to marry him until she'd had a chance to explore her career?

But then again, had she ever given him a chance? It was she who had walked away from the relationship without even discussing any possible compromises. She'd been so afraid of losing him to the pressures of her job, she'd thought it best to make a clean break of it from the first hint of trouble.

The thought chilled Lucy. But when she was

about to take a step backward, he stopped her, tightening his arms around her waist.

"No. Whenever I get too familiar or too personal, you retreat, either emotionally or physically." He brushed her hair back from her face. "Why, Lucy? Why can't you trust me?"

She opened her mouth, but no sound emerged. How could she explain to him something she didn't dare examine too closely herself, let alone put into words?

Nick seemed to sense her hesitance, because he drew her closer, holding her head against his chest.

"Trust me, Lucy. I would never do anything to hurt you."

Tears pricked at her eyes because she knew she'd hurt him. In refusing to marry him, she'd dealt a blow to his pride, his ego and his affections. And yet, after all that, he held her with the tenderness of…

Of a man who was falling in love.

No. He couldn't possibly love her. Not after everything that had happened between them.

But as she lifted her head to stare into the dark depths of his eyes, she saw a warmth there that could only mean one thing.

What had they done? In putting the past behind them, were they unwittingly making the same mistakes? Were they succumbing to their passions and closing their eyes to the obstacles that stood in the way of a true relationship?

Or was there more to their situation than that? Was the pull between them so strong that it was inevitable that they'd end up together?

"Do you trust me, Lucy?" Nick asked.

"Yes. Completely. If I hadn't, I wouldn't have come to you for help."

"Then can you continue to have faith in me? Can you give me a chance to show you that I would never hurt you?"

As much as she wanted to offer him an immediate affirmation, a part of her hesitated, because trusting anyone other than herself opened her up to the possibility of abandonment and pain.

But wasn't she hurting already? Wasn't she isolated and lonely? Hadn't she become so entrenched behind her emotional defenses that she'd found it difficult to feel much of anything anymore?

Until Nick Hammond had come back into her life.

"Yes," she whispered. "Yes, I think we both need to take a chance." She trembled in his arms, as much from the admission as from his nearness.

His smile caused her stomach to tense with renewed awareness.

Then his lips were touching hers again, softly, sweetly, slowly.

As the caress deepened, her lips opened beneath his exploration. With a soft sigh, the last of her resistance fled and she melted into him, surrendering completely to all that he offered—strength, passion, adoration.

He picked her up and moved toward the staircase. Resting her head in the crook of his shoulder, she closed her eyes, her fingers toying with the silky strands of his hair, her body thrumming with the desire that only he seemed to make her feel.

Once he'd reached his room, he closed the door with his elbow, then crossed to the bed in three strides, laying her on the duvet.

"You're sure?" he murmured as he stretched out beside her.

"Oh, yes," she said. "I need you tonight."

And every night, she longed to admit, but knew she mustn't.

Now wasn't the time for speeches or grand avowals of affection. Not when tomorrow could bring so much. Until she knew the twins were safe and well, her life would not be her own. Every decision she made would be influenced by their greater needs.

Thinking of the girls brought a renewed pang of fear. Needing to push such thoughts aside, if only for a little while, she turned to Nick, reassured that the baby monitor on his nightstand would let her know if the girls awakened. Eagerly, she reached for the buttons on his shirt, baring his chest and revealing the hard contours she'd admired during their nightly swims. Finally, she could explore each ridge and hollow to her heart's content, satisfying each lurid fantasy she'd had over the past few weeks.

But her forays were soon halted when he drew her own shirt over her head, then pulled her down. Excitement rushed through her veins like a heady wine. Every nerve, every muscle, became attuned to Nick until she could barely breathe.

When he rolled her onto her back, pressing her into the softness of the bed, she did not resist. For the first time in weeks, she was able to clear her mind of everything but this man, this moment. And even though she had no guarantees for the future, she knew she would forever treasure the memory of making love with Nick Hammond.

DAWN WAS JUST BEGINNING to tinge the sky pink when Lucy woke the next morning. For a moment, she struggled beneath a wave of confusion at finding herself in Nick's bedroom. Then the memories came flooding back, and with them an overpowering rush of fear.

Today was the day of the long-awaited surgery.

Although Nick was behind her, he must have

sensed that she was awake because he put his arm around her waist.

In the light of day, Lucy felt she should be stronger, but unable to help herself, she turned into his embrace, needing the last-minute reassurance that only he could provide. And when their desire bloomed again, slower this time, rich with emotion, she willingly gave in to temptation, making love with him yet again.

It was as she was showering that reality came crashing down on her. Had she completely lost her mind? She'd made love with Nick Hammond—and on the eve and morning of the twins' surgery.

Closing her eyes, she held her face up to the stinging stream of water. What had possessed her? She'd sworn she wouldn't allow their past history to complicate matters. Yet, within the space of a few weeks, she had surrendered to his magnetism in much the same way she had years ago.

Lucy groaned as the ramifications of her actions hit her full force. Despite everything that had changed between them, any sort of lasting relationship was still impossible. Moreover, she shouldn't have done anything to keep Nick from his rest....

Even with the water rushing over her, she could feel herself blushing.

Disgusted with herself, she shut the shower off and quickly dressed. Within fifteen minutes she was in the twins' room, gathering their things, then buckling their carrier into the van. Apparently Kyro and Tamika had already left for the hospital; they'd been given special permission to witness the surgery.

Her cheeks heated again. She could only pray that they didn't know where she'd spent the night.

"Ready?"

When Nick appeared in the doorway, she refused to look at him, even though she felt his presence with an enervating awareness.

"Yes, we're ready."

"Do you mind if we take my car? Since we won't be bringing the children home right away, we won't need the stroller and most of their paraphernalia."

Unspoken was the fact that Nick would undoubtedly be exhausted when he returned from surgery and the comfort and familiarity of the Mercedes would be appreciated.

"That's fine."

She allowed him to usher her outside, the twins and their carrier in one of his hands, the other resting on her back. Valiantly, she tried to ignore that spot of warmth and the goose bumps that appeared at his slightest touch.

After Nick had safely buckled the children into the back of his car, Lucy slid into her seat and the door locks clicked shut, accentuating the intimacy of the luxurious sedan. As the engine growled to life, her thoughts returned again to her worries.

How could she have made love with Nick? Had she lost all common sense? The situation with the twins was complicated enough without adding her conflicted emotions to the mix.

She closed her eyes against the bright light of the sun streaming through the window. Over and over again, she damned herself for her foolishness. By giving in to passion, she'd been able to push aside her fears, but now she worried that she might have distracted Nick when he needed to be at his most alert for the surgery.

"It'll be over soon." Nick said, and she started when he took her hand. "They're both strong."

"And they're fighters," she whispered, echoing the same words he'd offered before, her throat tight with emotion.

He lifted her hand to his lips. "I'll do everything I can for them, Lucy."

She looked at him then, absorbing the earnestness in his eyes, knowing that Nick would keep his word. He would do all he could to see that the operation was a success.

But there were many things that even he couldn't control.

"I'm sorry about last night," she blurted. "I

shouldn't have let it happen. I didn't have the right to distract you that way."

His lips twitched in a smile. "You're always a distraction to me, Lucy. Last night was no exception."

"Yes, but…I mean…"

Again, he kissed the back of her hand. "Don't regret what happened, Lucy. It was inevitable." She began to argue, but he continued. "I couldn't keep away from you any longer. I've tried, but so help me, you get in my blood and I can hardly think of anything else, night or day. But we'll talk about this later when—"

Nick had been pulling in to the parking lot, but he stopped suddenly, swearing under his breath.

"How did they find out about this?"

Following his line of sight, Lucy discovered a horde of reporters waiting by the rear entrance.

She sighed. "It was bound to happen, you know."

His eyes narrowed. "Are you implying that someone on the hospital staff—"

"No. I'm saying that the children are noticeably different, and it wouldn't take a genius to figure out why they've been visiting a renowned children's hospital. Once a single reporter got wind of the girls' situation, it would be easy to find out when the surgery was scheduled. And since the media grapevine is notoriously swift, I'd be surprised if the major networks *hadn't* shown up."

Nick grimaced. "And I thought we'd managed to keep things under wraps."

"Leave them to me. I know what to do."

Nick looked at her questioningly. "You're sure?"

"Drop me off in front of them. I'll take the children with me—they'll never leave us alone if they don't get a glimpse. While I'm doing that, park the car and head into the hospital. Warn security—but I'm sure they're already aware of what's going on. Let them know we'll hold a press conference after the surgery has been completed but that no information will be given out before then. Have the same information passed on to the switchboard."

Nick did as she asked, pulling up in front of the gaggle of reporters. Immediately, Lucy was recognized and they gathered around her. With some difficulty, she was able to remove the carrier and make her way to a spot near the front door. There, she made a brief statement about the twins' condition and the upcoming surgery, promised more details after the procedure was finished, then dodged inside amid camera flashes and shouted questions.

To her relief, a pair of security guards stepped up behind her to ensure she wasn't followed. In a minute Nick appeared, taking her arm and ushering her toward the bank of elevators.

"Nicely done," he commented with a smile.

"I'm a reporter—I know what they want," she quipped.

As the elevator door slid shut, Nick studied her with gentle eyes. "Yes, and you're very good at your work."

Of all the things she might have expected to hear, a compliment about her job skills would've been at the bottom of the list.

Lucy eyed the rapidly increasing floor numbers and knew she had very little time to say what was on her mind.

Impulsively, she reached for Nick's hand. "Nick, I'm sorry that I—"

He placed a finger over her lips to silence her apology. But before he had a chance to speak, the doors opened. On the other side were nurses and members of the surgical team who had clearly been alerted to their arrival.

Before Lucy quite knew what was happening, she and the children were swept away in the direction of the pediatric wing to stow the twins' gear before going down to pre-op.

When she glanced over her shoulder and saw Nick disappearing in the opposite direction, she was again assailed with fear, but she bit her cheek to keep herself from calling him back.

From this moment on, Nick was in charge of a delicate medical procedure and she couldn't do anything to ruin his concentration. Even from this distance, she could see his demeanor change to that of a complete professional—and it was as if she were staring at a stranger. Gone was the casual, relaxed air of a lover, and in its place was a focused leader. Turning away from him, Lucy tried to still the panic in her chest, knowing that from now until the surgery was over, she was on her own.

The next half hour was a blur. She helped dress the children in hospital gowns, then held and comforted them as intravenous lines were inserted into their tiny veins. She traveled with them as they were wheeled down to the pre-op room, all the while signing one consent form after another.

As soon as they arrived downstairs, the staff members began color coding everything that would make the trip into the O.R.—pink for Faith and green for Hope. Even the nurses and doctors wore clothing to match, signifying which child they had been assigned to help. Last of all, they used permanent markers to identify the girls themselves, drawing smiley faces on their hands and the bottoms of their feet.

Then, suddenly, Lucy was left alone to hold and comfort the girls in a cubicle that seemed inappropriately small and utilitarian. The air-conditioning vent overhead blew cold air against the nape of her neck, and she shivered, wrapping the children in a blanket so they wouldn't get chilled.

Tears filled Lucy's eyes as she whispered words of love to them and kissed the tufts of fluff on their heads. Again and again she told them they would be all right and this day would soon be over, but she knew she was speaking more to herself than to them.

Valiantly, she clung to the memory of Nick's arms around her and his reassuring words. But her emotions seesawed from joy—at giving the children the opportunity to reach their full potential—to desperation—because of the consequences the operation could have.

Closing her eyes, she prepared herself for all the complications that might arise. According to medical knowledge, it was the twin on the right who usually suffered most from the drastic surgery, and with Hope being the smaller twin, Lucy knew that was a distinct possibility. Even so, she worried for both of them equally. There could be excess bleeding from the liver, heart failure, a reaction to the anesthesia.

"Lucy?"

She looked up, the panic so strong she could taste it on her tongue.

"Yes?"

"My name is Rosa."

"Yes, we met once before. You're the nurse who'll update me from time to time during the surgery."

The woman smiled, her dark eyes filled with empathy. "I promise to keep you well informed." She hesitated a moment, then said, "It's time."

Lucy nodded. Woodenly, she stood. After more teary kisses she set the twins on the gurney. "Take good care of them."

"We all will. I promise." Rosa started rolling the children away and Lucy wanted to follow, but she knew she couldn't. "Do you know the way to the waiting room that's been set up for you?" the nurse asked.

"Yes."

"Good. I'll see you there in about an hour."

Chapter Eleven

Tears slipped down Lucy's cheeks as she watched the twins disappear behind a pair of heavy doors. Falling back onto a chair, she offered up a silent prayer for them and for the surgical team. Then, knowing that if she surrendered to her emotions completely she would spend the day stuck in a crying jag, she gathered her things and began to work her way through the maze of halls to a visitors' lounge that had been reserved for her use. In it was a battered couch, a recliner, a television, soda machine, several metal chairs and a castoff table holding a coffeemaker.

Sinking onto the recliner, Lucy leaned her head back and closed her eyes, clenching her hands in an effort to keep her imagination from running away with her. The moment the twins arrived in the operating room, there would be three teams of doctors and nurses waiting for them. One team, with Nick as the chief surgeon, would handle the separation. Two more teams would wait to attend to each of the babies after the separation was complete.

As pleased as she was that Kyro and Tamika had been given the opportunity to further their education, she started to wish she wasn't so alone. Maybe she shouldn't have agreed to the private waiting area. Even the company of other strangers would have provided some distraction from her thoughts.

A knock at the door had Lucy's heart pounding, her fingers gripping her chair. Were they coming to give her an update already? Something must have gone wrong, horribly, horribly wrong.

Almost immediately, a woman poked her head around the corner.

"Lucy? There's someone here who says she's a relative. She says she's come to wait with you."

The door opened wider and Lillian stepped into the room.

Lucy bit her lip, tears gathering in her eyes again. Her mother was pale, but her eyes were clear and her step sure, despite the aid of the cane she used.

"Mom?"

"Hello, sweet pea," her mother said, using the nickname she'd given Lucy when she was small. "I thought you'd like some company."

Lucy jumped to her feet and rushed to give her mother a kiss on the cheek.

Lillian reached up a hand, her skin smooth and velvety and smelling of her familiar White Shoulders perfume—a scent that Lucy always associated with her mother.

"I'm so glad you came, Mom."

Lillian smiled, her eyes sparkling in a way that Lucy hadn't seen in years. "You didn't think I could stay away on such a momentous occasion, did you?" She patted her oversize bag. "I brought a deck of cards to keep our minds off things. We can play hearts, penny a point."

Lillian sat down on the couch and Lucy took a seat next to her, marveling at her mother's lucid frame of mind and buoyant spirits.

"How did you get here?"

"I thumbed a ride on the highway."

When Lucy's mouth dropped, Lillian giggled— a sweet, girlish sound that made her seem years younger.

"Dottie, my day nurse, brought me."

"But—"

Lillian patted Lucy's hand to forestall any objections.

"Don't you worry about me. I know it's been a while since I've had an outing, but I've got Dottie's pager number and I can call the home if I need to. Right now, my place is here."

Lucy couldn't speak around the lump of emotion that lodged in her throat. But there was no need to say anything. Her mother dug into her purse, removing the familiar worn deck of cards she used for her games of solitaire. She shuffled the deck with the skill of a Las Vegas dealer.

"I don't know if I even remember how to play, Mom."

"Then prepare to lose your money. Mama needs a new pair of shoes."

THROUGHOUT THE SEEMINGLY endless day, Lucy became even more grateful for her mother's presence. Although they were periodically updated via telephone or by Rosa, those points of contact were interspersed with long, nerve-wracking bouts of uncertainty.

The first time Rosa appeared, Lucy clutched her mother's hand.

"It's taken a little longer than we thought, but the children are fully anesthetized," Rosa said, her mask hanging loose around her neck. "Just as planned, Dr. Hammond is working slowly and pausing often to give the girls time to react to the shock of the procedure."

An hour later she returned with, "The breastbones

were easily divided. The surgeons were relieved to discover the children shared less tissue than originally believed."

The next update came by telephone.

"They've reached one of the most critical portions of the surgery with the liver. It will be slow going for a while to minimize internal bleeding as much as possible."

Since her mother seemed to be getting tired, Lucy suggested she go home to rest, but Lillian refused, insisting she would just take a nap in the recliner.

Lucy found her a blanket. Then, needing an outlet for her anxiety, she propped the lounge door open in case she received another phone call, and began to pace up and down the hall, slowly at first, then with greater urgency, until her movements resembled a power walk. As she paced, she watched the clock on the wall. The minute hand inched its way along until it had been fifteen minutes. Thirty minutes. An hour.

Expectantly, she waited for the ring of the phone or the whisper of Rosa's bootie-clad feet on the tile, but she didn't hear anything for another thirty minutes.

When Rosa finally came around the corner, Lucy ran to meet her.

"What's happened?" she asked anxiously.

Rosa drew her into the lounge and sat on the edge of the couch, pulling Lucy down to sit by her.

Lucy's heart pounded, dread filling her mouth with a bitter taste.

"Everything is stabilized, but we encountered some problems. Dr. Hammond said to tell you that on reaching the liver, he discovered there was a natural plane of separation where the two livers had fused. It took about an hour, but he was able to make the cuts with a minimum of bleeding…"

"But…" Lucy prompted when Rosa hesitated.

"We had a bit of a scare when Hope's respiration and her oxygen levels dropped and she went into distress."

Lucy couldn't suppress the cry that burst from her lips.

"How is she?"

The question came from Lillian who had awakened and was gripping the blanket with white knuckles.

"She's stable again. Dr. Hammond stopped the surgery for a while and her body recovered on its own with the respite."

"And now?" Lucy whispered.

"The surgery has already resumed and Hope is holding her own, but we'll continue to watch her closely." Rosa squeezed Lucy's hands. "I'll be back as soon as we've reached another milestone, but it might be more than an hour. Why don't you and your mother go down to the cafeteria and get something to eat."

Lucy shook her head. "I couldn't possibly—"

Lillian quickly interrupted her. "If we called the volunteers' desk, do you think they could bring something here?"

"That's a wonderful idea," Rosa said. "You'll see their number posted next to the phone."

Rosa disappeared again, leaving Lucy trembling and wondering how close they'd all come to losing little Hope.

Lillian leaned forward to take her hand. "Don't torture yourself over things that might have been," she said firmly. "Take it from me, it isn't worth the effort. Count your blessings and focus on the fact that both of the girls are still with us."

Lucy nodded, clinging to her mother. "I don't know how much more of this I can take," she whispered, her nerves drawn so taut she thought they'd snap.

Lillian stroked her daughter's forehead. "Nonsense. You're a strong woman—stronger than I ever was. And you've got Nick Hammond to shoulder the burden, don't forget that."

Yes, Lucy could rely on Nick. He would do everything he could to help the children. She merely had to trust him.

Trust him.

In the past, Lucy had been leery of letting anyone else have any control over her life. But in this situation, the choice had been taken away from her and she discovered that it wasn't nearly as painful as she would have thought. There was a comfort in knowing that she wasn't alone. She had her mother. And she had Nick.

The man she loved.

The thought was so sudden and so powerful that it was like a lightning bolt shooting through her system. But with her defenses already weakened, she knew she could no longer deny the truth.

She was in love with Nick Hammond.

And in that moment, he held more than her own life in his hands.

NEARLY FOURTEEN HOURS after he'd entered the operating room, Nick touched the scalpel to the last remaining piece of tissue that connected the twins. He couldn't have counted the number of times he'd prayed for a successful conclusion to the surgery. At one point, when Hope had gone into distress, he'd worried that this moment might never come. But now, six hours after Hope's body had managed to stabilize, he made the final cut, and all the tension and strain shifted out of his body as if it were sand, leaving him weightless.

The twins were now two separate individuals.

"It's done."

Clearly, the other teams had been waiting for those words because they sprang into action, moving Hope to her own separate gurney, and from there to an adjoining operating room where the plastic surgeon's team would have more space to work. Tamika and Kyro automatically split up, one remaining with Faith and the other staying with Hope. At the same time, Nick backed away so that Faith's plastic surgeon could take his place.

They'd done it. The girls were alive and fighting for their chance in the world.

"Would you like me to call Lucy and her mother?" Rosa asked at his side.

Nick shook his head. He had an opportunity to take a small break before supervising the rest of the surgery, and he wanted to be the first to tell Lucy the good news.

"How much longer do you think it'll be?" he asked the surgeon who was carefully drawing the skin into place over Faith's chest.

"An hour, maybe a little more. The other baby might be a bit longer since she has less skin to work with and we'll have to take things slow. Then we've got belly buttons to form."

"Okay. I'll give the news to their mother myself then meet you in the recovery room."

It wasn't until he'd walked through the swinging doors that Nick realized his mistake. Out of habit, he'd spoken of relaying the news to the twins' "mother."

But even as he mulled over his slip of the tongue, Nick knew he hadn't been completely wrong. Legally Lucy might only be the children's guardian, but from what he'd seen of the love and attention Lucy lavished upon them, she could clearly be considered their mother.

So what would become of them when Lucy left?

Not wanting to think about that, Nick tore off his mask and gloves, disposing of them. Then he arched his back and stretched out the kinks in his shoulders. It had been a long day. A long but rewarding day.

Stepping out into the hall, he made his way toward Lucy's waiting room. He could only imagine what agony she'd suffered throughout her forced exile. While the time had seemed to fly for Nick as he concentrated solely on the task at hand and the condition of his tiny patients, she must have endured the torment of her own imagination.

At least he could reward her with some good news.

When he rounded the corner in the corridor, Lucy was pacing in the opposite direction. Then she turned and marched toward him, her gaze intent on the tile at her feet. Within a few yards, of Nick she must have sensed his presence because she paused, her expression a mix of anguish and hope.

"The separation is complete. The plastic surgeons are closing up now and should be finished in an hour or two at the most."

"And the girls?" she whispered.

"They're holding their own. They'll be in ICU for some time, but their vitals are steady. You know all the problems that could still arise with possible infections and postoperative complications, but…"

"But they're going to make it," she said, throwing her arms around his neck. "They're going to make it!"

Sobs of joy mingled with her laughter, the sounds drawing an older woman from the adjoining room. Nick instantly remembered her from the one time he'd met Lucy's parents.

Seeing Lillian, Lucy held out her hand. "Mom, they're going to be all right!"

Lillian's eyes grew bright with tears and she clapped her hands together, then held them in front of her mouth.

"When can we see them?" Lucy asked, turning back to Nick.

"I'd like to keep them in recovery at least until the anesthesia is showing signs of wearing off, so it'll be a few hours before we take them upstairs." His eyes narrowed. "Have you eaten today?"

He knew by the stain of pink in her cheeks that she hadn't.

"They brought us some soup and sandwiches, but we couldn't bring ourselves to eat," Lillian admitted.

"Go to the cafeteria now and get something hearty," Nick said sternly. "There's nothing you can do for a few hours, and I know you'll want to stay near the girls once they head up to ICU."

Lucy hugged him again. "Thank you," she whispered close to his ear.

As she backed away, taking Lillian by the hand and leading her down the hall, Nick felt an unaccustomed tightening of his chest.

Never in his life could he remember when someone's gratitude had touched him so deeply. He was infinitely thankful that, if nothing else, he'd been able to help Lucy and her girls.

A LITTLE OVER TWO HOURS later, Lucy looked up as Rosa entered the waiting room.

Since Lillian was clearly exhausted, Lucy had insisted she return home. Then, her stomach filled with a comforting bowl of hot soup and a huge chef salad, Lucy had returned to the surgical wing.

"They'll be going up soon. Nick said you'd probably want to go with them."

Lucy immediately jumped up and started gathering her things. "Yes, I would."

They hadn't even reached the end of the corridor when the first gurney appeared. Rushing forward, Lucy felt tears spring into her eyes when she saw Faith.

She was alone.

The sight of the baby was at once beautiful and heartrending. Lucy had been so accustomed to seeing the twins together that to find one of them lying by herself amid a sea of tubes and monitors was shocking. It was as if Lucy were being introduced to the children all over again.

She kept watching the bed as it was pushed toward the elevators. Then the operating-room doors swung open and there was Hope—so tiny, so vulnerable, so wonderful.

Lucy cried even harder, realizing that her first glimpse of them was like witnessing their birth. She hadn't been there to see them come into the world, but she was here now to see them emerging from the operating room as two separate beings.

As they stepped into the elevators and the doors slid closed behind them, Lucy bit her lip. Now that she was mere inches away, she wanted to touch them, to reassure them that she was there, but she didn't know if she should. The girls were swollen and covered in bandages. Besides, the tubes and monitors discouraged any sort of cuddling.

Seeking some unhindered portion of their bodies, she settled on stroking their feet. So many challenges still remained. The fact that they had survived the surgery didn't mean that an easy road lay ahead. Lucy knew the medical staff would be on the lookout for signs of infection, respiratory distress, liver failure, kidney failure, even cardiac arrest. So many of their internal organs had been directly or indirectly affected by the separation.

But Lucy also knew that the babies had been strong enough to come this far—and the strength they had displayed would serve her girls well in the future.

Her girls?

The thought caused Lucy to grow still. When had she begun to think of the girls as hers?

She unconsciously shook her head in warning. Such possessiveness was dangerous. The twins weren't hers and they never could be. As much as she might want to adopt them, she didn't have that right. Her lifestyle wasn't conducive to any kind of family.

The elevator doors opened, revealing Nick and a

group of nurses waiting on the other side. As the beds were wheeled away to the ICU, her glance slid to Nick. A wave of sadness tugged at her heart. It wasn't even possible to keep a romantic relationship alive under the demands of her career, let alone become a mother.

But in a moment of illumination, she understood that it wasn't her job that had kept her from completely committing to a relationship. It was her own fears. She'd always believed that she would be unhappy in such a traditional role and would just end up making everyone else miserable.

But she'd loved playing the role of the twins' mother. Staying at home with them had been more rewarding than she ever could have dreamed.

Firmly closing off her mind and emotions to the longings that threatened to overtake her, Lucy followed the twins as they were rolled into a corner of the room and the monitors were taken from the beds and placed on more permanent stands.

Enough. She was too tired and overcome with emotion to think of anything but this moment. Tomorrow would be soon enough to worry about the future.

NICK WATCHED in pride as Lucy stroked the girls' tiny feet and whispered into their ears. The strain of the day was beginning to pulse through his body, but the high he was experiencing from the success of the operation made any sort of rest impossible.

Yet, despite his good mood, his emotional guard was down. As he stared at Lucy, the depth of his feelings stunned him. He'd willingly admitted he was still attracted to her. He'd even acknowledged that he'd never completely stopped loving her, that she still aroused a passion in him that was fierce and undeniable.

But he couldn't be *in* love with her. He wouldn't allow himself to make that same mistake twice. Lucy would wither and die if she was forced to stay in one place, while he…

All of a sudden, Nick wasn't quite so sure why things couldn't work between them. Experiencing a rush of shame, he realized that in the past he may have given the impression that he'd expected all or nothing in his relationship with Lucy, that he wanted a woman whose career wouldn't interfere with his own. Now he could see that by being so unbending in his views, he had erected a shield to protect himself from true commitment.

In fact, Nick realized that he'd sabotaged all his relationships. He had purposely dated strong, career-oriented women, subconsciously knowing that none of them would place their affection for him ahead of their work. In doing so, he'd been able to convince himself that it was never his fault that things didn't work out.

On the heels of his sudden epiphany came a second wave of shame. By his actions, he had denied himself so much. And yet, he also felt a glimmer of hope because he now realized that he was ready to build a lasting bond with a woman, no matter what it took.

Still, he hesitated to pursue Lucy. The danger that she courted in her job scared him. His life and his career were demanding. How could he add fears about Lucy's safety to the mental and emotional challenges he already faced each day?

But even those worries paled beneath his overriding concern. Nick could deal with her job, the dangers and the crazy schedule. But only if he knew that Lucy could truly give herself to him, heart and soul, without keeping anything back.

Could he ever work his way beneath the last of her defenses? Could he ever figure out what made Lucy close a part of herself off? Did he even want to try?

Without a doubt, he knew that he did. Suddenly, nothing mattered more than to set Lucy free from whatever demons possessed her—even if it still didn't guarantee he'd get her back.

Chapter Twelve

In the days that followed, Lucy was relieved that all the attention centered on the children and their recovery. Nick was spending long hours at the hospital. And she…

She was spending most of her time with the girls. Between the three of them, Lucy, Tamika and Kyro provided a constant presence for the babies so that they would never feel alone. Lucy spent hours rocking and cuddling them, or simply sitting by the cribs in case the children needed her. Yet, in those moments when she was by herself, her thoughts invariably returned to Nick.

Grateful that the twins were okay, she was also happy to take a break from the intensity of her relationship with Nick. Heaven only knew that she had to clear her head in order to make some difficult decisions. And she couldn't do that if Nick continued to pursue her.

If he even wanted to pursue her…

His hours had been so unpredictable that she'd rarely seen him outside the hospital. The regular news briefings to the media had inspired a great deal of interest in the hospital and Nick's team, and they'd been besieged with inquiries about children with special medical needs.

So Lucy had been left to her own devices for the most part. Which was a relief, she insisted to herself again.

Wasn't it?

"Hello, everyone."

At the sound of Nick's deep voice, every nerve in Lucy's body came alive.

After everything that had happened since she'd arrived in Utah, one would think that Lucy would've grown accustomed to Nick's presence, but the second he entered the room, her body invariably had the same reaction.

Breathing deeply to quiet her nerves, she listened with half an ear as Nick spoke with the nurses in charge of the ICU.

In addition to the twins, Nick had three other patients in the unit, but it was clear that he was spending a lot of personal time here, as well.

Lucy felt her cheeks flush, knowing that the children weren't the only reason for his visits. Since making love with Nick the night before the surgery, it had become obvious that he wanted to be around her as much as possible.

And she had a feeling it wasn't mere physical intimacy he sought. If it were, Lucy was certain she'd be able to resist his advances. But no, he seemed to value her company, their quick conversations, the chance to squeeze her hand.

She lowered her head to cuddle Hope as the baby slept against her chest.

While Faith seemed to be recovering rapidly, Hope was still struggling to hold her weight and temperature. She'd been placed on a respirator soon after leaving the operating room, but within twenty-four hours, her vitals had been steady, if weak. Nevertheless, in the two weeks since her surgery, she'd made continuous small steps toward improvement, and Lucy remained optimistic about her recovery.

Nick looked down at his clipboard.

"Their blood work's looking quite good this morning."

"Both girls'?"

He nodded, flipping through the pages. "Much better than yesterday. Hope's white count is back to normal, so I think we've been able to head off the signs of infection she began showing a couple of days ago."

This time, Lucy's exhalation was one of relief.

Nick smiled and peered into the crib beside him where Faith was trying to bat at the colorful mobile the nurses had placed just beyond reach. "As for Miss Faith, here, she's gained a whole pound. Since both girls are doing so well, I've arranged for them to be transferred out of ICU to the intermediate nursery."

He put down the clipboard and regarded Lucy with undisguised affection. "And how are you this morning?"

What was it about this man that he had only to look at her with those warm, dark eyes for her thinking skills to deteriorate completely?

"I—I'm fine, I guess."

His eyebrows rose. "You guess? You mean you don't know?" He leaned close and brushed a kiss over her lips, murmuring for her ears alone, "Trust me, you're fantastic."

Then, before she could gather her scattered thoughts, he was moving past her, about to finish the rest of his rounds.

Leaning her head against the back of the rocker, Lucy closed her eyes.

What was she going to do? Despite the fact that she'd promised to trust Nick Hammond, she couldn't seem to control the panic that was building inside her. The twins' health was improving every day. It wouldn't be long before Lucy would be forced to find an adoptive family for them. According to the stipulations made when the children were allowed to enter the country, they would need to be placed for adoption within the year or be returned to Zaire. As soon as they were placed with a family, Lucy would no longer have a reason to stay in Utah.

Biting her lip, she fought back the tears that such thoughts inspired.

She'd known the time would come when she would have to give the twins away. So how had she allowed herself to become so attached?

But even as she asked herself the question, she knew it would've been impossible not to develop a close bond with the children. They were living, breathing miracles—and they'd brought her more joy than she ever would have imagined.

Just as Nick had done.

Damn, damn, damn. Although falling in love with the children had been unavoidable, she should have been more careful about letting her feelings for Nick grow to this extent. She'd warned herself…

So why hadn't she listened? Why had she allowed herself to care so deeply?

And what was she going to do about it now that she was head over heels in love?

"Lucy?"

She started, her eyes springing open to find one of the nurses standing in the doorway.

"There's someone here to see you."

Knowing that visitors were discouraged from coming into this section of the hospital, Lucy stood and gently placed the sleeping baby back into her crib. It still gave her a bittersweet rush to see Hope lying on her back all alone. Although it was wonderful that Hope would now be able to grow unhindered, she seemed so lonely and vulnerable without her sister's larger body to cradle her.

After removing the sterile gown she had to wear while she held the girls, Lucy made her way to the waiting area beyond the nurses' station.

As soon as she set foot inside, a plump, motherly-looking woman got up from her chair and rushed toward her.

"Miss Devon?"

"Yes, I'm Lucy Devon."

The woman beamed, her brown eyes sparkling. "Matilda Redmond."

Lucy shook her proffered hand.

"I hope you'll forgive me for approaching you this way. I'm an adoption facilitator for an agency here in Salt Lake." She reached into the portfolio she carried and removed a card. "I had a baby who was released to his adoptive parents today and while I was completing the paperwork, the hospital's social worker happened to mention that you'd been given my name as a referral. Since I was in the building, I thought I'd introduce myself."

The hairs prickled at the back of Lucy's neck. "I…I see. Thank you."

Her guardedness must have been obvious because Matilda lifted her hands. "Don't misunderstand me. I'm not trying to force my services on you. But the social worker said you had some very pointed questions about adoption and the procedures for placing a child. She suggested I might be able to help."

Lucy's brain seemed to seize up, coherent thought becoming impossible.

"Would you care to join me for a cup of tea or a cold drink from the cafeteria? I've been here since early this morning, so I could use a dose of caffeine. I'd love to sit and just talk if you'd like."

Lucy felt as if her extremities were turning to stone, but the woman had such a homey, maternal aura about her that she nodded. "Yes, I'd like that. Just let me get my purse."

WHEN SHE LET HERSELF into the house later that evening, Lucy was exhausted, emotionally and physically.

Although she'd been leery of Matilda Redmond and the information she had to offer, she'd known that she needed to talk to the woman. Lucy had already delayed starting the adoption process much too long. The time had come to at least educate herself on the matter.

But after they'd treated themselves to tea and pie from the hospital cafeteria, Lucy had soon discovered that Matilda was easygoing and concerned only with being a sounding board for Lucy.

What began as a formal interview soon melted into relaxed conversation, with Matilda offering a wealth of experience and insight into adoption. In the end, she'd been able to alleviate Lucy's fears, assuring Lucy that she was in control of the entire process. Lucy would be able to interview families, meet them face-to-face and even discuss with them the sort of relationship she might be able to have with the girls in the future.

But as she kicked off her shoes and padded toward the kitchen, Lucy didn't feel as relieved as she should have been.

"So I heard you met with Matilda Redmond today."

Lucy stopped short as Nick appeared in the

kitchen doorway. He raised his hands, gripping the molding around the frame. It should have been a re-laxed pose, but there was something about his stance that betrayed him.

Lucy sighed, raking her fingers through her hair. "Yes. I spent a few hours with her. I was able to get a lot of information."

"She's a good woman. I've worked with her sev-eral times over the past few years."

Tension flooded around them. Not the heady sex-ual tension Lucy was accustomed to feeling when Nick was near. This time it was the taut anticipation of a confrontation.

"Did you two make any decisions?" Nick asked after a moment.

Lucy shook her head. "I just asked her about the adoption process in general."

"I see."

Nick finally lowered his arms and stepped back, allowing Lucy to pass. She headed to the cupboard for a glass, added crushed ice from the refrigerator door, then cold water. Sipping, she moved to the window, knowing that Nick was still waiting to hear what she'd discovered and how she planned to pro-ceed from here.

"What should I do, Nick?" She glanced at him over her shoulder, meeting his dark gaze. "I promised the nuns I'd find permanent homes for the twins—it was a stipulation agreed upon when their emergency visas were granted. I can't let the sisters down. It was imperative to them that the girls be placed with loving families."

"It's not as though they've been starved for love," Nick said, his features composed in a careful mask.

"No, but the attention we've given them is no substitute for something permanent. They deserve that much and more. Faith and Hope need a stable home, two parents, a picket fence, a dog."

His lips twitched. "I think they're a little young to be worrying about a dog."

"You know what I mean. I want the best for them. And according to Matilda Redmond, there are dozens of couples just waiting for a chance to give them everything they could possibly need."

"But…" he prompted.

"But…I can't seem to make myself take the necessary steps to put things in motion."

"Then maybe you should keep them."

The words were softly uttered, echoing the whispers of her heart. But hearing them aloud didn't make the idea any more feasible.

She sighed. "And what kind of life would that be? I'm on the road more than half the year. They'd have to be left with nannies or paid caretakers. That's not what the sisters had in mind—and it's not the best thing for them."

"Then let me adopt them."

The words dropped with the weight of a large rock. Lucy could not have been more stunned as the rippling reaction to his statement washed through her system.

"What?" she asked in disbelief. Surely she hadn't heard him correctly. Nick couldn't possibly be thinking of becoming a father to the girls.

"Let me adopt them," Nick continued quickly, his expression so earnest that it took her breath away. In that instant, he looked younger and more alive than she could ever remember. "I've been thinking about it for a long time. I love the girls. I can't imagine what it would be like if they weren't around. This house would seem so big and empty without them. Granted, they won't have a mother for the time being, but there are a lot of advantages to the arrangement. Faith and Hope would be with someone they know, someone with an intimate knowledge of their condition. They would have constant access to medical care and a stable, loving home. I think I could even persuade Tamika and Kyro to stay on. They've expressed an interest in continuing their education and this would be an ideal situation for all of us."

For all of us.

Except her. There'd been no mention of Lucy in any of these arrangements—but why should she be surprised? She'd just insisted there was no room for motherhood in her future, that it was time she went back to the life she'd once led.

Yet, the hurt at being excluded, even if that had not been Nick's intent, was so profound that she could hardly breathe.

Nick moved closer, taking her arms, determined to press his case. "They would be happy here. They'd have good schools, access to parks and playgrounds—"

She took a step backward to release herself from his grip. Stiffly, she said, "I'll think about it. But right now…"

Her throat was tightening with emotion, but she refused to let Nick see that she was upset. She had nothing left but her pride, and she would cling to it with every ounce of strength she had.

"I—I need to shower and change," she said. Then, turning on her heel, she hurried in the direction of her room, knowing that if she stayed, she would break down completely.

She managed to strip off her clothes and get underneath the stream of hot water before she started weeping uncontrollably. More than anything, Lucy wished she could keep the future at bay, but she knew she'd already stalled for as long as she could.

The girls were on the way to recovery. If all went well, they would be released from the hospital in a few weeks. At that time, it would be better for them to begin their new lives with their adoptive family.

Lucy's head pounded. As much as she might want to keep them herself, she couldn't. One day soon, she would have to return to work. She couldn't leave them with a nanny. They deserved more than that. And what would happen if they suddenly became sick or suffered complications due to their surgery? How could a nanny be expected to deal with such problems?

Which left Lucy with two choices. She could call Matilda Redmond and begin the search for a family.

Or she could allow Nick to adopt them.

Sagging weakly against the shower wall, Lucy knew there was no real debate. Nick might not be married at present, but the opportunities he could offer the children both medically and personally far outweighed that detail. More important, he'd formed a bond with the girls, and they responded to him with patent eagerness.

Lucy squeezed her eyes shut as she was again overcome with a wave of sadness. But this time, as the tears coursed down her cheeks, mingling with the warm spray, her grief was for herself alone. The children would be loved wholeheartedly. She had no doubts about that. Nick would care for them as if they were his own and they would never want for anything.

But Lucy doubted she would fare so well. By placing them with Nick, she would be losing a part of herself—and she would always hunger for the might-have-beens.

Lucy turned off the water and numbly reached for a towel. Then, moving into the bedroom, she sank onto the edge of the bed and reached for the phone. Her fingers trembled as she punched the buttons.

Hurry. Hurry before you change your mind.

"CNC, Frank Carlisle's office."

"Nan, this is Lucy Devon. If Frank is still looking for a replacement for Parker, I'll go to Colombia."

NEARLY AN HOUR had passed before Lucy could control her emotions enough to begin making the arrangements for her departure. She called her lawyer to begin drawing up the adoption papers. Next, she connected with the news team already in place and the cameraman who'd be meeting her at LAX and traveling with her to Colombia. She packed her bags and arranged for part of her belongings to be shipped back to her apartment building in Chicago, where a fellow reporter who'd been subletting her suite would put them in storage. Then, after making her travel reservations online, she closed her laptop.

Her hands were trembling so badly that she tucked them between her legs and the seat of the chair.

"I can do this," she whispered to herself. Then, more forcefully, "I *have* to do this. There's no other choice."

Lucy's one consolation was that she knew she'd be able to visit the girls from time to time. It was a condition she would insist upon—and one she didn't think Nick would begrudge her.

Now, the only detail that remained was informing Nick of her decision.

Ironically, when Lucy went searching for him, she found him in the nursery. He was conferring with Kyro about the twins' latest test results.

Lucy poked her head in the door. "Could I speak to Nick privately for a moment?"

Kyro shot a quick glance at each of them. "But of course. I'll just go help Tamika with dinner."

"Thank you."

Lucy waited until Kyro's footsteps had faded before stepping all the way into the room and shutting the door behind her.

"Is something wrong?" Nick asked.

"No. Not at all." Lucy shoved her hands inside her

pockets then, knowing that she'd never be able to speak if she looked at him, went and stood over by the window.

Outside, sunlight glinted off the pool's surface. Bright flowers surrounded the patio with a blaze of color. The lawn had been newly mowed, and clumps of mature trees offered inviting patches of shade in which to escape from the day's heat.

This would be a perfect home for two little girls. Lucy could already envision a swing set and playhouse in the backyard, and toys and tricycles left leaning against the rocks of the retainer walls.

"Were you serious when you offered to adopt the children?" Lucy asked. She refused to face Nick. Nevertheless, she felt the power of his regard.

"Yes. I was very serious."

Lucy bit her lip, then continued before she could change her mind.

"Despite the problems we had with our own relationship years ago, I want you to know that I never blamed you for anything. It was *my* decision to leave." Lucy took a steadying breath before adding quickly, "You're a good man, Nick—and I know I can trust you to do what's best for Faith and Hope. That's why I think you should adopt them."

He remained silent for so long that she was finally forced to turn and look at him.

"Are you sure?" he asked softly.

"I've known all along that I couldn't take care of them myself. As much as I've grown to love them, my lifestyle simply isn't what's best for them. They need stability and access to constant medical supervision." She swallowed. "For weeks, I've been trying to find my way out of this predicament. It was your offer that finally gave me the peace of mind I needed to make a decision."

Nick seemed to be stunned. Obviously, he hadn't expected her to consider his suggestion at all, let alone agree to it in less than an hour. Lucy knew it would take time for him to adjust to the fact that he had just become an instant father of two.

"I've arranged for my lawyer to come by this evening with the papers. I'll sign them before I leave in the morning."

Lucy brushed past him, intent on seeking out the safety of her room. But she'd barely made it to the doorway when he stopped her by saying, "This isn't right, Lucy."

She froze, glancing over her shoulder. "You told me you wanted them," she said. "Have you changed your mind?"

"No, I haven't changed my mind. There's nothing in this world that I would like more than to become their father. But…"

"But what?"

"Not like this."

"I don't understand. Everything will be legal."

"But you can't make a decision like this in haste. You have to be sure this is what you want."

"I *am* sure." She cleared her throat to rid her voice of a betraying quiver. "I want the best for them, and that means letting you adopt them."

"And what about you?"

She'd wanted to iron out those details when she wasn't so emotional, but clearly Nick planned to discuss them now. "I'd hoped that I'd be allowed to visit them a few times a year."

"Nothing more?"

Her fingers curled into tight fists. What more could she have than that? "No. I wouldn't want to interfere with your new family. I only want to be able to see them. Now, if you'll excuse me, I have some packing to do. I'm leaving for Colombia tomorrow morning."

He laid a hand on her arm.

"Wait until you come back before you do anything final. The girls will be fine here, it'll give you a chance to think, and—"

"And what? Nothing will have changed. My life will still be the same—hectic, demanding and sometimes dangerous. While yours will be…peaceful."

She wrenched her arm free. "I've made up my mind, Nick. Unless you've decided you don't want to adopt the children, we really don't have anything more to say."

His eyes glittered—and for a moment his expression was so close to the one he'd worn when she'd left him at the courthouse five years ago that she shuddered.

"Fine. Run away."

She gasped. "I am *not* running away."

"Aren't you?" This time he pulled her around to face him. "Do you know that for the last five years you've haunted me like a ghost? Consciously or unconsciously, I've compared every woman I've ever known to you and they've all come up lacking—not because they weren't wonderful women, but because they weren't *you*."

"No," she whispered hoarsely. "Whatever you've done or not done in the past five years is your problem, not mine."

"Yes. You're right. I've made my own life and I've been happy. But with all my success, there were still times when I wondered, *Why?* Why didn't things work out between us? I'd convinced myself that it was your fault more than mine, that you'd chosen your career over our relationship.

"But I see now that we were both to blame. We

ignored the differences between us instead of working through them. And we relied on passion to hold everything together but that wasn't enough. I was so focused on my own career that I didn't take your career seriously.... No. That's not right. That's the easy answer. To be honest, I was jealous of your work, and the time, energy and dedication it would involve. I didn't want to be second in your life—and I knew your job would always come first."

She trembled, her very world shifting beneath her at Nick's admission. Yes, at the time her job had been more important to her than this man. But now...

But now...

"And it wasn't just your job that sabotaged us, Lucy." He stroked the sensitive inside of her elbow, causing goose bumps to race up her shoulders and raise the hairs at the back of her neck.

His eyes darkened with bittersweet remembrance. "Why, Lucy? Why wasn't I enough for you? What were you running from that made you turn away from me long before you showed up at that courthouse to announce you wouldn't marry me?"

His words pierced her to the very core.

Running from? She hadn't been running away from anything. She'd been running *to* something. She'd been consciously choosing a life of travel and adventure.

Chapter Thirteen

As Lucy climbed into the taxi and gave the driver directions to the Jaeger Convalescent Home, she worried about how her decision to go to Colombia would affect her mother. Lillian's condition had improved steadily over the past few weeks. She was now interacting with others around her and seemed happier than she'd been in years. Could the news that Lucy was leaving cause a relapse?

Lucy wasn't foolish enough to think that she'd had very much to do with her mother's improved state, though. The children were the ones who'd helped her the most; it was as if they'd brought out the loving side of Lillian, which she'd been afraid to express while her husband was alive.

Lucy didn't resent the fact that her mother was able to convey more emotion to the twins than Lillian had ever displayed with her. Lucy's own experiences had helped her to understand and empathize with her mother's demons. She could only pray that Nick would continue to bring the children to visit Lillian during her absence. Her mother needed to see them as much as possible before Lucy signed the relinquishment papers.

Relinquishment papers. Why did that term have to sound so...awful?

If she was forced to tell the truth, Lucy would have to admit she was relieved her attorney had called to reschedule their appointment due to a conflict in court. He'd seemed more comfortable with the delay himself, stating he thought she might need more time to think about her decision before she committed to anything.

So why hadn't she insisted on signing the papers before she left?

Because I couldn't bring myself to take that step. Even though I know it's the right thing to do, I can't let the girls go just yet.

Staring out the window, Lucy realized within hours she'd be back to her old life. Yet, rather than feeling relieved and uplifted for having brought the twins this far, her spirit was decidedly battered and bruised. Until that morning, she hadn't realized how impossible it would be to say goodbye to Tamika and Kyro, the children—and Nick. Leaving him, knowing he was watching her from his upstairs bedroom window, had nearly killed her.

The taxi slid to a halt next to the front doors and Lucy said, "Can you wait? I'll just be five minutes."

"Sure. But I'll need to keep the meter running."

As she hurried into the reception area, Lucy glanced at her watch. She really shouldn't have taken this detour. She was supposed to be boarding in ninety minutes, and she still had security to navigate. Indeed, in the past, she would have done anything to avoid spending time with her mother. But lately…

Lately, she'd needed her mother's quiet support.

Lucy tapped on Lillian's door and let herself in. Her mother was sitting in her customary chair by the window. For one heart-stopping moment, Lucy feared that she'd returned to one of her foggy states. But Lillian turned her head and her eyes lit up at seeing Lucy.

"Hello, dear! What brings you here this time of day?"

Suddenly overcome, Lucy rushed toward her. Kneeling on the floor, she rested her head on Lillian's knees, hugging her, offering an anguished explanation about her trip. But the words didn't stop there. In a torrent of emotion, she told her mother of her love for Nick and her attachment to the children.

It was only when she felt her mother stroking her hair that Lucy looked up to discover Lillian's eyes were filled with tears.

"I am so sorry, sweet pea," Lillian whispered. "It's my fault."

Lucy shook her head. "Mama, none of this is your doing."

Lillian put a finger to Lucy's lips. "No. I know what I'm talking about. It's my fault that you're so guarded. I gave you the wrong impression when you were younger."

She stroked Lucy's face, her gaze taking on a far-away expression as if she were seeing the child that Lucy had once been. "I know now that I was ill—emotionally more than physically. I surrendered to my disappointments instead of railing against them, and in doing so, I punished you for something that wasn't your fault."

"No, Mama. You wanted more out of life and Daddy wouldn't allow you to—"

Again, Lillian laid a finger over her lips. "No. You see, even that was a smoke screen for what really hurt me. It wasn't the loss of my dreams that filled me with bitterness. It was knowing I was in love with a man who would never love me in return." Her fingers trembled against Lucy's cheek. "I was a fool and a coward. Rather than divorcing your father and following my dreams, I stayed and stewed in my misery, punishing everyone around me."

This time, it was Lucy's turn to comfort her mother. As she held Lillian in her arms, Lucy suddenly saw her childhood years through new eyes. She'd always thought it was the loss of her mother's chance at a career that had caused her to be so miserable. But now Lucy could see that her father's coldness had caused far more damage, sapping her mother of the confidence to strike out on her own.

A sudden knock on the door had them both looking up.

A freckle-faced nurse stepped inside.

"Lucy, your taxi driver asked me to check with you. According to the radio reports, there's been an accident on the freeway, and he's worried about getting you to the airport on time."

"Thanks."

The nurse closed the door and Lucy turned back to Lillian.

"I don't want to leave, Mom."

"I know, sweetie."

"I'll come visit as soon as I get back. In the meantime, I'll call as much as I can and I'll ask Nick to bring the girls by to visit."

Lillian stood with her and walked her to the door.

At the last moment, Lucy hugged Lillian close.

It was the first time she could remember ever doing so before leaving her mother. As a family, they'd never been demonstrative. But so many things had happened to tear down those barriers, and Lucy couldn't have left without whispering, "I love you, Mom."

"And I love *you,* sweet pea. I am so very proud of my little girl. Don't ever forget that."

Knowing her control was limited, Lucy turned and strode out into the hall. Ignoring the curious glances she received from some of the staff, she wiped at the tears streaming down her cheeks and pushed through the double glass doors to the blast of heat outside.

"Let's go," she said as she slid into the cab.

"Yes, ma'am."

Normally, Lucy was prone to engaging strangers in conversation. She had developed some of her most interesting stories from chats with ordinary people doing ordinary jobs. But right now, she knew she couldn't speak. Nor could she concentrate.

She could only ache with a pain unlike any she had ever felt before.

She needed to get a handle on her emotions. The flight to L.A. would take little more than an hour. As soon as she landed at LAX, she would meet up with the rest of her crew. It was imperative that she be in complete control of herself and the situation. She couldn't break into tears at the mere thought of…

Two beautiful little girls.

Nick.

A mother who was proud of her.

Squeezing her lashes shut, she pressed the heels of her hands to her eyes.

What was the matter with her? She was about to participate in a once-in-a-lifetime story. As soon as she arrived in Colombia, she would shake off the last vestiges of her life at home, just as she had so many times before. The thrill of the assignment would quickly replace whatever heaviness still lingered in her heart. She would become consumed with the need to outscoop the other news agencies bent on covering the same story.

Lucy let her hands drop and she gazed sightlessly out the window.

Why was leaving suddenly so difficult? She'd spent her life running away…

No. She hadn't been running *away* from anything. She'd been running *toward* adventure, knowledge, enrichment. She'd been eager to shed her real life for…

Shed her real life?

Then her reporting had been an escape from—what?

Family?

Commitment?

Unhappiness?

No. It was more complicated than that. She loved her job. It was an integral part of her identity.

But it could never make her completely happy.

The whisper from her conscience was so unexpected that Lucy held her breath for a moment, then released it.

Balance. It was all a matter of balance. Many women were able to handle it all—marriage, children, a career. But Lucy had always known that—personally—she could never juggle that many balls. So now, after having conquered the challenges of her job, she was discovering that she wanted something else.

Something more.

She didn't want to go on this assignment. It didn't matter that it was a once-in-a-lifetime opportunity. In a moment of epiphany, Lucy saw that her entire career had been a series of once-in-a-lifetime stories. And as much as she'd loved every minute, the dangers involved had taxed her to the limits of her physical and emotional endurance.

It had taken Faith and Hope to bring her to this realization. By taking these few months off to do other things, Lucy had discovered that there were other challenges she longed to tackle.

Such as committing herself to a relationship.

Being a mother.

Lucy bit her lip as she absorbed the depth of what she was contemplating. She was thinking of contacting Frank Carlisle at the last minute and bailing out of an assignment that could very well be one of the top stories of the year.

It could be done. She only had to make a phone call. Frank would be furious, but he'd recover soon enough.

And if she stayed in Utah, then what?

Her stomach tightened nervously. If she stayed, there would be no running from Nick or the fact that their relationship had reached a crossroads. He deserved that much. She would either have to make a commitment or withdraw.

Old familiar fears rose to the surface, and with them memories of her childhood. She'd sworn that she wouldn't become like her mother. She wouldn't let her independence be taken away from her.

But her memories were quickly overshadowed by her most recent conversation with her mother.

Lillian had *chosen* her fate, it hadn't been foisted upon her.

For so long, Lucy had been running away from her past, afraid that she would end up trapped in a permanent relationship and that her identity and her very soul would be swallowed up by her husband.

But she suddenly realized what Lillian had been trying to tell her: She could only become a martyr to her destroyed dreams if she let it happen.

Yes, her work was an important part of who she was. But she had followed that path to the exclusion of all others. And if she denied herself this last chance at love, she would be far unhappier than Lillian had ever been.

It was her choice.

The thought was accompanied by a sense of peace and a sense of purpose.

Her choice.

Lucy could continue to the airport and pursue a story that most reporters would have killed for—

Or she could stay in Salt Lake and be a mother to the children.

Yes. Yes!

Lucy tapped impatiently on the glass barrier. "I'm sorry. We'll need to go back to the same place you picked me up."

"I'll have to wait until the next exit to turn around. You don't have much time…"

"That's fine. Just go as fast as you can." Now that her decision had been made, Lucy couldn't wait to go…home.

Digging into her duffel bag, she took out her phone and punched in Frank's number. To her relief,

Nan Tarkington answered and informed her he was in a meeting.

"As soon as you can, let him know that I can't go to Colombia."

"What?" The normally shrill voice on the other end of the line sounded that much more strident.

"I've had a family emergency. I can't go."

"But—"

"I don't have time to explain now. Just tell Frank that I'm sticking to my original plan to take six months off. After that time, I'll let him know what kinds of assignments I'll be ready to handle."

"But—"

"Oh, and you won't be able to reach me at this number, nor will I be returning any calls for at least three months, so make sure Frank knows that I won't be changing my mind."

"But—"

Lucy didn't even bother to listen to any arguments that Nan might make. She snapped the lid shut, rolled down the window, then threw the phone onto the road. To her utter satisfaction she saw the device hit the pavement, then shatter into a thousand pieces.

The driver was watching her in the rearview mirror, but other than raising his eyebrows, he didn't comment.

As she relaxed in her seat, Lucy grinned. She felt

only a twinge of guilt. She knew full well that a dozen other reporters would be waiting in the wings to jump at this opportunity. Frank would be angry, but even that didn't worry her. She simply had to believe that she'd made enough of a name for herself that she could find work elsewhere if need be. Who knew? Maybe by then she would decide to teach. Or write. She'd always wanted to write about her experiences.

Joy engulfed her. She was closing one avenue of her life for the time being, but she was beginning to see the myriad other directions she could take. Yet none of those options appealed to her as much as telling Nick that she loved him.

As the cabdriver maneuvered to a stop at the curb, she handed him the fare and a hefty tip and gathered her things.

"Don't you want me to wait?" he asked in confusion.

"No, thanks. I've changed my mind about going."

He blinked, then nodded his head as if he suddenly understood. "Aaahh. Fear of flying, hmm?"

She grinned, "No, I'm conquering my fears by staying instead of going."

He looked at her in utter bewilderment, but she didn't bother to explain. Nudging the door shut with her hip, Lucy hurried up the front walk.

So much had changed since that first night when

she'd come up this same path. The twins were strong and healthy. And as for herself…

She felt as if a huge weight had been taken from her shoulders. More than that, she felt happy. Completely and utterly happy.

This time, when she reached the front door, she didn't bother to knock. Instead, using the key Nick had insisted she keep, she let herself into the house and dumped her bags in the foyer.

Lucy listened for any sound that might signal Nick's whereabouts. A smile spread over her lips as she heard the betraying rush of the shower overhead.

It was funny the way life sometimes went full circle.

Moving as quietly as she could, she took the stairs and crossed through Nick's bedroom to the master bath. There, behind the steamy glass, she saw the outline of a familiar form—the broad shoulders she'd caressed, the arms that had held her.

Leaning against the doorjamb, she studied him for a satisfying minute. And then, as soon as he'd turned off the water, she said, "Hello, Nick."

Nick froze, his arm still extended toward the handle of the shower door. As if he were trapped in slow motion, he pushed the glass aside.

"Lucy?"

Moving slowly toward him, she took a towel from

a nearby hook. Once she was but a few inches away, she gently wiped the moisture from his face, his shoulders, his chest.

"Did you miss your flight?"

The words were so carefully uttered that she rose on tiptoe to kiss his chin.

"No. I didn't get as far as the airport."

"Is something wrong with your mother?"

"Not at all. She seems better every day."

She saw the pulse in his neck quicken.

"Then why are you here?"

He posed the question so softly, she might not have heard it if she wasn't standing so close.

Knowing she couldn't contain her feelings another second, she met his gaze and whispered, "Because I love you and I can't go away."

As soon as her confession was out, she found she couldn't hold back her emotions any longer. Throwing her arms around his neck, she offered him a disjointed explanation of why she'd returned. She prayed she wasn't too late, that he hadn't already decided he was better off without her.

But just as she ran out of ways to convince him that she was sincere, his arms wrapped around her waist and he hauled her close.

"Dear God, Lucy, I love you, too. I don't know what I would have done without you."

In that instant, as she absorbed the heat of his body and the strength of his love, Lucy knew she'd made the right decision. Life was a gamble—and she intended to bet her happiness on a future with this man. He wasn't anything like her father and she'd been wrong to measure Nick with that yardstick. Nick loved her; he didn't want to own her. If she'd left him and abandoned their relationship, she would have regretted it forever.

Nick released her only enough to frame her face with his hands. He paused, then said, "I want to marry you, Lucy Devon. And if you'll consider it, I'd still like to be the father of your children."

Her eyes filled with tears, but she blinked them away. She wanted to remember this moment and the tender expression on Nick's face for the rest of her life.

"There is nothing on earth I want more," she answered, hoping that he would see her heart in her eyes.

His whoop of joy could probably be heard on the next block. Embracing her tightly, he whirled them around and around. Then he carried Lucy from the bathroom to the bedroom, placing her on the bed and hovering over her.

"I'll hold you to your promise," he whispered with a grin.

"It's a promise I won't break this time."

His grin widened. "You can count on that. I don't intend to let you out of my sight until we can say our vows. I'm also intercepting all of your calls."

She laughed. "There's no need for that. As soon as I realized I was making the biggest mistake of my life by leaving, I begged off the assignment, then threw my phone out the window."

Nick stared at her in astonishment. "You can't be serious."

She stroked his cheek with her finger. "It's true. As we speak, I-215 is being littered with little bits and pieces of electronic circuitry."

Nick bent, kissing her softly, sweetly, lingering over the caress as if memorizing every facet of her. Then, leaving only a hairsbreadth of space between them, he whispered, "I know how much your job means to you, Lucy. If you want to traipse to the far corners of the earth on dangerous assignments, I'll find a way to deal with it. Just…"

She stopped him with a finger to his lips.

"Right now, you and the children are all I need. There's nowhere else I'd rather be than with all of you. Maybe, in a year's time, I'll be ready to go on assignment again. But my years of living dangerously are over. I've got too much to lose."

Her hands moved over his shoulders and down his spine. She knew that sometime soon she'd have to explain to him everything she'd learned about herself and her fear of commitment. But for now, she wanted to feel his arms around her so she would know this moment was real.

After that?

Well, after that, they'd have a lifetime together to figure out the details.

Epilogue

"ARE THEY READY?" Nick asked, his hand resting tenderly on Lucy's shoulder.

"Just about."

Lucy carefully maneuvered Faith's chubby fist through the sleeve of a hand-knitted sweater adorned with violets. Then she straightened to study the two little girls who lay side by side.

It was still a marvel to see the twins this way—separate, individual. Yet today, the effect was even more special. For the first time since entering the hospital, they'd been dressed in street clothes—tiny jeans and flowered T-shirts topped by the adorable sweaters. The matching outfits—one with violets, one with roses—had been going-away presents from the nursing staff.

Lucy tugged a pair of matching knitted hats over the girls' heads and slipped soft shoes onto their feet. "There, that should do it."

She handed Faith to Nick and he carefully placed the baby in one side of a brand-new tandem baby stroller. He did the same for Hope, then asked, "Time to go?"

Lucy nodded and grinned. "Yes. It's time to go."

Slinging the diaper bag over her shoulder, she preceded Nick through the doorway of the intermediate care nursery to the nurses' station beyond.

When they emerged, the nurses applauded, quickly gathering around the stroller to offer their congratulations—both to the children and the newly married couple. The women oohed and aahed over the circlet of diamonds that Nick had placed on Lucy's finger in the hospital chapel minutes earlier and the men slapped him heartily on the back.

Slowly, Lucy and Nick made their way through the pediatric wing downstairs to the lobby where more doctors, nurses, technicians—and Lillian—waited to see them off. Saying goodbye to the many professionals who'd helped bring this moment to pass was difficult. Emotions ran high. There were tears and laughter and even a good measure of boasting. But as Nick wheeled the children into the sunshine, Lucy knew they would return often to see the caring staff. There would be many follow-up visits in the months to come—and a special first-birthday party had already been planned by the nurses. In time, the children would need further cosmetic surgery to their chests and abdomens. But for now…

For now, they were like any other family, strolling from the hospital, going home.

After helping Lillian into a cab, they installed the children in a new minivan purchased a few days earlier. Lucy couldn't deny that she was happier than she'd ever been. The twins were growing stronger with each day that passed. Lillian Devon—who had fallen in love with Nick as much as she had with Faith and Hope—seemed to have found purpose in her new role as the twins' grandmother. She'd gone on her first shopping trip in years to find a dress to wear to Lucy's wedding and had insisted on staying with the children for two days while Lucy and Nick took a whirlwind honeymoon next weekend. Tamika and Kyro were ecstatic over the turn of events, as well, since they'd be continuing as the children's nurses for a few more months, and also beginning part-time jobs at the hospital.

But what made Lucy's joy complete was knowing that her husband loved her, body and soul.

"What's made you smile like that?" Nick asked, dropping a kiss on her nose as he reached around her to open the passenger door.

"You," she said simply, sliding into her seat.

As Nick stowed the stroller, she leaned her head

back, reveling in the warmth of her husband's adoration. She wasn't naive enough to think that they'd never argue, or that their marriage would be without its bumps. Nick's uneasiness with her job would still create challenges—as would the ghosts from her upbringing. But Lucy was so certain of the depth of commitment between them that she knew they could weather such storms.

The shadows were growing long when Lucy and Nick entered the house with their little family. Since Tamika and Kyro were working the nightshift, the newlyweds were alone as they fed and bathed the children, then tucked them into their cribs. Leaving the baby monitor on, they climbed the stairs to their own bedroom for their long-awaited wedding night.

"I love you, Lucy Hammond," Nick murmured.

"And I love you," she sighed, pulling him close.

Their lovemaking was slow, sweet, and full of the elation of that day. And later, when Lucy was about to fall asleep with her head resting on her husband's chest, a faint smile settled on her lips. Beneath her ear, Nick's heart beat in time with her own—much as the twins' hearts had done before their separation.

"That's nice," she whispered sleepily.

She only vaguely felt Nick stroke her arm as an exquisite drowsiness swept over her.

"What is?" he asked, his voice a rumble under her ear.

She yawned, nestling deeper into his embrace.

"The way you have my heart," she whispered, not really making any sense as she fell asleep.

But she didn't need to explain. As he drew the covers up around her shoulders and switched off the bedside lamp, Nick knew exactly what his bride had been trying to say.

Finally, they were together…the way things were always meant to be.

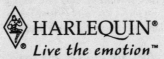

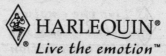

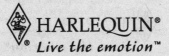

If you enjoyed what you just read,
then we've got an offer you can't resist!

Take 2 bestselling love stories FREE!

Plus get a FREE surprise gift!

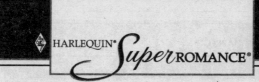

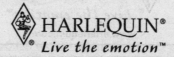

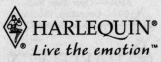

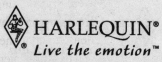